RYANN FLETCHER

Bearly Together

This book was professionally typeset on Reedsy.
Find out more at reedsy.com

To anyone who's ever found family in an unexpected place.

Contents

Chapter 1

December was a strange time in Roanoak Falls. While most of the country was hoping for a white Christmas, residents of Roanoak Falls had been dealing with snow for months already. Wren loved the cold, but not the weeks-old muddy snowdrifts that cluttered the parking lot of the store.

She kicked a clump of dirty slush off her boot, sending it to land on the sodden mat with a wet splat. The words, *Welcome to Joe's*, were barely visible underneath the thousands of muddy boot prints.

"You're late. Everything okay?"

"Sorry, the bus ran late."

"Coffee's in back. Don't forget to clock in."

"Thanks."

He tapped his thumb percussively against the flip phone holstered on his belt. "You're quiet this morning.'"

"I'm just tired," Wren said with a yawn. It was already one of those days, and she hadn't even clocked in yet. "I'm just going to drop my things in back and get an apron."

"Maybe two cups of coffee for you, then."

"Alright, Mr. Ranelli." She unzipped her thick parka. "Maybe even three cups."

Wren twisted the soles of her winter boots against the black mat that ran along the single register, wiping whatever was left from outside to melt away against the rubbery underside. She'd have to mop later. She used to love winter and Christmas, but this year felt flat and uninspiring. All of the cold, none of the wonder or awe, or even a passing reminder that people weren't as bad as they seemed. Pushing through the employees only door, Wren's hands caught on a staple sticking out of the wood. The single lightbulb in the room flickered, casting odd shadows across the old, paint-chipped desk.

She sighed, kicking off her heavy boots and slipping on the black flats from inside her shoulder bag. Her worn coat looked at home hung on the rusty hook, unlike the lumpy, oversized apron that she tied around her waist.

"I'm heading out for lunch," Joseph Ranelli called from the front of the store.

Wren looked at her watch. Nine-o-seven. "See you this afternoon, then."

"Sales numbers for today are on the back wall. Try to shift some of those upscale shop vacs, will you?"

"Sure thing."

The bells on the door jingled merrily as he left, and Wren scowled. *Sales numbers*, she thought. *Give me a break.*

The residents of Roanoak Falls weren't easily swayed by sales tactics, and she'd never met someone who could be talked into buying a five hundred dollar wet and dry vacuum that they didn't need. Mr. Ranelli would no doubt give her a sad, defeated smile when he returned from his five hour lunch, lamenting that the store hadn't sold out while he was gone, despite there being no one to sell *to*.

"What shall we do today, then?" she asked the large inflatable snowman that loomed near the door. "Busywork as we slowly slide into a pit of despair?" She paused. "Yes, I think that sounds just fine."

Irritatingly cheerful holiday tunes eked out through the speakers, popping with static. The sound system, if you could even call it that, was probably as old as the building, and there was no way Mr. Ranelli would replace them. "People don't come here to listen to the music. We're not an entertainment venue," he'd said.

Wren sighed again and poked at a few boxes of fuses on the end display, pushing them towards the front of the shelf. When that was done, she moved to re-organizing the endless trays of nuts and bolts, all in different sizes, and all of them mixed up. No doubt Mr. Ranelli's grandkids had been in again, tossing things around. At least it was better than shoveling the parking lot.

She scowled at the sky through the doors. It was grey and crisp, the perfect kind of weather to dump more snow over the town. Thick, fat flakes that would accumulate themselves into piles of heavy precipitation. The forecast had said no snow, but she knew that was rarely a guarantee.

Mopping might as well get done. At least if she did it earlier, it was out of the way, then. She dragged out the old yellow bucket from the closet and began to fill it with hot water from the tap in the utility sink, suds from the detergent rising faster than the liquid.

"Hello?" a voice called from the front of the store, the bells jangling with no harmony.

Wren wiped her hands on her apron. "Good morning, Mrs. Pennington."

She gave a demure smile, her perfect loose curls cascading over her shoulder like a brunette waterfall. She unzipped her name-brand polar fleece vest and laid a hand against her curvy hip. "Darling, if I've told you once, I've told you a dozen times, call me Amber."

"Is there anything I can help you with today?" Wren was glad for the distraction, and truth be told, it could have been a worse customer. She'd nursed a crush on Mrs. Pennington when she'd first moved to town.

"Hmm... lightbulbs, I think."

"They're just at the front, there."

Mrs. Pennington - Amber - glanced around theatrically. "Can you show me?"

"Uh, sure." Wren dunked the dirty mop back into the bucket, leaning it against the white pegboard wall. She shuffled to the front of the store and gestured towards the aisle lined with lightbulbs. "They're just here. What kind did you need?"

"Oh, one of everything, I should think."

"I'm sorry?"

"I want to make sure I'm prepared. I can't remember every bulb type in my house, you know!" Mrs. Pennington flashed her a bright, white smile. "And I wouldn't dream of getting them from anywhere other than here."

"Oh, yeah? And why is that?"

"Because I feel that I have a duty to shop local, of course. It's just not the same at the big place across town."

"Mr. Ranelli will be very pleased to hear that."

"You should tell him that you deserve a raise, while you're at it."

Wren barked a laugh. "Sure thing."

"I mean it!"

"I'm sure you do, but I doubt that will change his mind any time soon."

Mrs. Pennington smoothed her chic pantsuit. "Perhaps he will change his mind when I am mayor."

"You're running for mayor?"

"Of course, Wren. I can't stay PTA president forever. Lean in, I always say." She pulled a large stack of pamphlets from her oversized bag. "Here, you can have these, if you want."

"I don't know that Mr. Ranelli—"

"Oh, I've known him for years, I'm sure he'll be alright with it." Mrs. Pennington shook the floppy stack of papers. "Maybe you can hand them out to customers? Every little bit helps, you know! No rest for a mayoral candidate, that's the truth."

Wren took the stack and set them on the counter next to the register. "When did you decide to run?"

"Oh, a couple of weeks ago. Did you know that most state senators started off in local government?"

"No, I didn't."

"It's true! A verified, tried-and-tested path to success. Now that the kids are a little older, and they have so many activities, I just have so much time on my hands that I don't know what to do with. Idle hands are the—"

"Was there anything else you needed, Mrs. Pennington?" Wren held out the basket stacked full with lightbulbs.

"You know, I could use some help on my campaign team..."

"I'm not sure I have the time, with work, and... more work."

"It would be such a good experience for you! A pretty young thing like you could go far in this world, you know." Mrs. Pennington arched a perfectly shaped eyebrow. "There's always room for you at my table, if you change your mind."

"Thank you."

"Just these bulbs then, dear, if you don't mind. Need to make sure the house is brightly lit for the campaign open house! It's next weekend, potluck. Maybe..." she trailed off, biting her lip. "Maybe you'd like to come with me as my special guest."

"Oh, uh... I'm working." It was a lie, but a believable one. She couldn't stomach a party, not this year. "Sorry."

"I'll just have to talk to Joe about that then, won't I?" Mrs. Pennington said with an exaggerated wink. "He can't make you work all the time, you know."

"I don't think he—"

"Nonsense, Joseph and I go back decades. Besides, he owes me a favor. Someone got his name on the official suppliers list for the school's science fair. You can't put a price on that, now can you?"

Wren looked around at the empty store. "You sure can't," she agreed. "I really should get back to mopping. Mr. Ranelli will be back soon."

"Then perhaps I'll wait for him here with you, then I can tell him how you begged me for an invitation to my campaign launch. What do you think?"

"Mrs. Pennington—"

"*Amber.*"

"Yes, Amber, I don't want you to feel like you have to do me any favors. I'm sure you're busy enough with your campaign preparations without having to worry about my work schedule."

"It's nothing, Dollface. You know, the kids said they really miss you babysitting." She paused. "I do, too."

"They're getting all grown up now, aren't they?"

"That doesn't mean you can't come around. Between Suzy's debate club and Jon making varsity lacrosse as a freshman, it gets awfully lonely in that big old house alone sometimes."

"Does it?" Wren started to scan the boxes of lightbulbs, placing each one neatly into a tall paper bag. "I'd think a little bit of peace would be a good thing."

"Not for me. I hate being alone. I'd much rather have company."

"To each their own, I suppose. I've spent so long sharing an apartment that if I had a house like that, I wouldn't want to look at anyone for at least a month. Maybe a year."

"You say that now, but age and loneliness creep up on you fast, Wren. Ten minutes ago I was a young thing like you, running after my little ones. Now look at me, older, wiser, and no one to show for it."

"I wouldn't say that."

"My kids will be grown soon, off at college, exploring new things, making lives for themselves. Suzy wants to head out to the west coast, Jon to the east coast. Where does that leave me, other than in a flyover state on my own, rattling around in that big house?"

"It might leave you as mayor?"

"Exactly! Now you get it. So you'll come to my campaign launch?"

"I'll try," Wren lied. There was nothing less appealing than getting dragged to a political launch party, especially in a small town like Roanoak Falls. The presidential election had nothing on local politics, and the campaigns felt almost as long. "But even if I don't make it, you have my vote." She scanned the last box, setting it into the bag with some extra paper for cushion. "Your total is thirty-three fourteen."

"Prices have sure gone up lately."

"Inflation?"

Mrs. Pennington laid two crisp twenty-dollar bills on the counter. "Keep the change. A tip, if you will."

"I'm not allowed to accept tips."

"What Joe Ranelli doesn't know won't hurt him."

Wren nodded her head towards the security camera. "He'll know."

"Then I'll have to owe you one. How about that?"

"Really, that's not necessary—"

"Don't be silly, Ms. Jackson, I know good service when I see it. You absolutely must let me make it up to you. How about dinner?"

Free food was hard to pass up, and Mrs. Pennington—Amber—was very persuasive. "I won't say no to that."

"When do you have a night off?"

"This Thursday."

"Stupendous, we'll go to the little Thai place on Main Street. I'll pick you up at eight." Amber gently lifted the bag from the counter, resting it against her hips, clad in expensive blue linen. "I deeply look forward to it."

The door closed, and Wren sighed, reaching for the mop handle. She might as well waste a couple of hours pushing dirty water around the floor. It's not like there was anything else better to do.

Chapter 2

The leafless trees were skeletal against that afternoon's grey, pressing sky. Another crappy little town, another assignment from corporate.

"Don't forget to send over that data, Monroe. We're all counting on you."

"I'll send it as soon as I'm somewhere with internet."

"Where are you at, anyway? I'd have thought you would have arrived hours ago."

Monroe dragged her hands over the smooth leather of the steering wheel. "Almost. Ran into a pileup on the interstate." She squinted at the house numbers glued to bent mailboxes. "Just let me unpack, Steve, and I'll get back to you on those numbers, alright?"

"Hopefully, this place doesn't put up too much of a fight. I know some of us have seen some opposition in the Midwest."

"Looks small, but I don't anticipate any problems. Anyway, in and out, right?"

"Counting on you, Chase. If we don't get this signed and sealed before December twenty-fifth, we'll all be working overtime."

"Don't worry, I bet I'll have it done by the end of the week."

"I look forward to seeing those reports."

The line disconnected, leaving Monroe in the relative silence of the car's engine, quietly idling. She twisted the key and sat staring at what was meant to be her house for the next few weeks. A cute, quaint place, if a little outdated, and a far cry from her modern apartment she kept back in the city.

Wind rustled through the dead tree limbs, and she shivered. There was snow in those clouds. She could feel it burning just beneath her skin.

"No," she said aloud, and snapped a rubber band against her wrist. "No."

Pulling her plain black suitcase from the trunk of the car, she rolled it along the driveway, the wheels protesting against the poorly maintained concrete. There was a note taped to the glass storm door on the porch.

The key is hidden under the plant pot.

Monroe couldn't help but smirk at the trusting naivete of the owners. Maybe this neighborhood didn't have a problem with theft. Still, she turned and pressed the lock button on her key fob, just to be safe, the rented car letting out a quiet, dignified hoot. The house key was exactly where the note said it would be, sitting flush against the white wood boards of the porch.

The house had a distinct country feel to it, with shiplap on half the walls and a sliding barn door closing off the living room from the rest of the house. She kicked off her stylish shoes, sending them to clatter against the hardwood floors. The white curtains were crisp, the folds from when they were in the packaging still running through them like a knife. This hadn't been a rental for long, and the strangely empty frames along the hallway proved it.

She carried her suitcase upstairs, dropping it on the bed and unzipping the sides to hang her clothes in the derelict closet. Insufficient packing was always a powerful motivator to get the job done and get out before schedule. It's why she'd been promoted three times in the past eighteen months, and was one more expansion contract away from a regional management position.

The second bedroom was a makeshift office, with a flat pack particle board desk and a chair that barely looked like it would hold her weight. Still, it was enough, and she didn't plan on staying long. Monroe laid her laptop on the surface and bent, looking for the wi-fi router. All she found was an ethernet port.

"Damn listing said it had internet," she grumbled to herself. "Who doesn't have wi-fi these days?"

With an irritated sigh, she headed back down the stairs, her thin socks sliding on the wood. She took a quick glance at the kitchen, which was predictably empty, before grabbing her keys and stuffing her feet back into the boots. Back into the wilderness of wherever the hell she was. Monroe snatched the paperwork from her open briefcase. Roanoak Falls.

* * *

She pulled into the parking lot of the only hardware store she could find that wasn't part of a Syndicorp superstore. Just because she worked for them didn't mean she had to give them back her hard-earned money, and besides, this was closer.

"Hi, welcome to Joe's," came a bored voice from the back of the store. "I'll be right with you."

"Oh, don't worry, I can find it myself." The store was packed with stock, some boxes stacked nearly to the ceiling. Racks of wallpaper, bins filled to the brim with nuts and bolts, and snowblowers along the back wall. No doubt those got a lot of use in a place like this.

Monroe scoured the shelves, looking for an ethernet cable. "You don't have wi-fi routers here, do you?"

"What? No. This is a hardware store, not an electronics store." A woman in a shop apron poked her head around the corner. "Best I can do is an ethernet cord."

"That's what I came here for."

"You're in luck," she said, pulling a grey package from the next aisle. "This one is thirty feet long. That enough?"

Monroe blinked. "Er—yes." The woman was cute in that kind of artsy way, her hair tied around her head in an intricate braid, a small hole in the side of her cable-knit sweater. Monroe coughed to cover the silence, turning her gaze back towards the cord in the woman's hand.

"Did you need anything else?"

"What's it like to live here?" Monroe asked. She hadn't meant to, but the words slipped right off her lips.

"I don't know. It's fine. It's just a normal town, like anywhere else."

"The snow doesn't bother you?"

"Not the first few times in a season, but it gets old having to shovel, you know?" The woman tugged at her apron, revealing a nametag. Wren. "Why?"

"Just curious, I suppose. I'm just passing through."

"If I were you, I'd leave as soon as possible."

Monroe took the package, turning it over in her hands. "That's the plan, more or less."

"I was *going* to say, as soon as possible, unless you really love nerdy festivals and hot chocolate. In that case, you should check out the town square later."

"I don't think I'll be here long."

Wren twisted a ring around her index finger. "You got family here, or something?"

"No, no family. Not here, anyway. They live overseas. I travel a lot, so don't see them much."

Wren tilted her head. "I'm sorry."

"Don't be."

"Was there anything else you needed?"

"I don't know. What else do you have?"

"Ugly wallpaper?"

Monroe laughed. "I think I'm all set on ugly wallpaper."

"How about an enormous, illuminated reindeer?"

"I don't know if I can commit to that level of outdoor seasonal enthusiasm."

"Hmm," Wren said, tapping her fingers against her chin. "I can also offer you a drain snake."

"I sincerely hope I don't end up needing one of those, I'll be honest."

"No one *wants* to need a drain snake, but you're happy to have one when you do."

"A fair point."

"So, what do you do? What brings you to Roanoak Falls?"

"Er…" Monroe trailed off, searching for the right answer. Some people didn't take well to the truth of her employment. "I'm a land surveyor for a big company. I look for places where they can open new stores."

"Sounds boring."

"It is, mostly."

"Good thing you're not from Syndicorp. Joe would have such a tantrum if one of them showed up."

Monroe stared. "Uh, yeah. Good thing."

"Plenty of people here aren't keen on them, you know?" Wren shook her head, letting loose a strand of hair from the crown of braids around her head. "It's hard enough to keep this place going, without that kind of competition."

Guilt burned in Monroe's stomach. "I bet."

"So what kind of store will it be? Ooh, or will it be a restaurant? We could really use a bookstore here, or... never mind."

"No, I'm interested now. What?"

"A bakery?"

"What, like, wedding cakes and pastries?"

Wren smiled, and it was like the sun was beaming out through her eyes. "Yes, but also loaves of bread, cupcakes, tarts, that kind of thing. It would be so beautiful, don't you think? All lined up in the shop window, the smell of sugar and flour drifting out into the street."

"Seems like you've thought about this a lot."

"Nah." She leaned against the edge of the aisle. "Anyway, it doesn't matter. Your store isn't going to be a bakery."

"No, it's more of a... general store. Of sorts."

"Sounds quaint."

"Sure."

Monroe had the cord in her hand, but didn't want to leave. Something was keeping her rooted to the spot, despite the painful rippling at the base of her spine. "How long has this place been here?"

"Thirty years or more. Family business. Not mine—if I owned this place, there's no way I'd be walking the store trying to sell upmarket shop vacs."

"Shop vacs?"

"Yeah, you know. Lots of people have them in their garages for various jobs. Can clean wet or dry. Popular for car detailing and basements." Wren nodded over her shoulder. "Joe thinks I can sell one today. I'm wondering who the hell is going to waltz on in here and randomly buy a shop vac."

"I'll buy one." The words spilled out of Monroe's mouth before she even had time to think.

"You? Why? I thought you were only here for a short time."

"A gift for a... friend."

Wren laughed, her hazel eyes crinkling delicately at the corners. "Who buys a friend a shop vac for Christmas?"

"She, uh... really wants one. She told me so. Last week."

"Right. Well, we have three models, the—"

"I'll take the most expensive one."

"You don't even want me to explain the features?" Wren asked, an eyebrow arched.

"I trust you."

"Bold of you to trust a hardware store employee who has a vested interest in upselling you on unnecessary features."

"You have an honest face." Monroe bit down hard on the inside of her cheek, willing herself to stop saying ridiculous things.

"That's definitely a new one. Well, I'll just grab it and take it up to the register for you."

"That would be great, thank you."

Wren lifted the box onto a flat bed cart, dragging it towards the front of the store. "I hope your friend really likes her new shop vac."

"She's really into her car. Now she can detail it herself."

"It certainly isn't my hobby, but it takes all kinds, I guess."

"What is your hobby?" Monroe asked, and immediately regretted it when Wren looked at her, startled.

"I, uh... I don't know. Kind of. It's complicated."

"Are you part of a secret society, or something?"

"Yes, I'm actually part of a conspiratorial cult bent on overturning the government with shop vacs and ethernet cords. Your total is three-eighty-seven even."

Monroe slid her card across the counter, the matte black finish dull against the scuffed grey register mat. "Credit."

"You must really like this friend. No one has ever spent that on me for Christmas, not even that girl I dated for four years."

"Yeah, we're... really close."

The receipt printer screeched and coughed. "If you want to return it for any reason, you'll need the receipt. Joe doesn't allow no-receipt returns."

"I'm sure it will be perfect."

"How long are you in town for?"

Suddenly, she didn't want to leave Roanoak Falls. "I'm not sure, actually. Until the job is done."

"Well, from a townie, I recommend the Sparkling Lights festival. It's cheesy, but it's good for killing some time. They also have great funnel cakes."

"I don't think I've eaten a funnel cake since I was little."

"Opportunity abounds, then!" Wren tucked the stray lock of caramel-colored hair behind her ear. "Enjoy your time here, anyway."

"I think I'm starting to enjoy it more than I thought I would."

Chapter 3

"Wren, the gas bill is due. I left it on the table."

"Thanks," she grumbled in response. Another day, another bill, and her roommate was just as hard up as she was. "How bad is it?"

"Let's just say if one of us gets an offer to sell our soul for a few hundred bucks, we should probably consider it."

"Jaime—"

"I'm kidding. Mostly. But the weather has been garbage, and even with setting the thermostat low, it's still running more often than not."

"I assume you're still opposed to the plan where we just slowly freeze to death?"

"Listen, life might be shitty right now, but I have all the faith in the world that someday I'll win the lottery, and I want to be around to rake in the spoils."

"You don't even play the lottery."

Jaime shrugged. "You gotta have dreams. How was work, anyway?"

"Work was work. Joe took a five-hour lunch. I swear he must be going somewhere other than to the diner."

"The usual, then?"

"Yep." Wren picked up the gas bill and flinched. Her half was sixty-five dollars. "You know the bill wouldn't be so high if the landlord would put in new windows."

"I know, but try explaining that to him. The man squawks and screeches like I'm skinning him alive if I so much as mention it."

Wren sighed. "I can pick up some weather stripping from work."

"That shit never works as well as it says it will."

"Better than nothing."

"What's for dinner?" Jaime asked. "I'm starved."

"By the emptiness of the refrigerator, my guess is that our options range somewhere between pasta without sauce or a butter sandwich."

"That is wildly depressing."

"You're telling me," Wren replied, closing the fridge. "I forgot we ate the rest of the casserole."

"'Tis the season to overindulge on three-day-old casserole, I guess." Jaime smiled at their own wry humor. "How much have you got in your account?"

"I don't know, enough for rent and my half of the gas bill, probably. Maybe bus fare if I'm really rolling in dough."

"Let's go to the diner."

"What about any of what I just said suggests that I have enough to eat out?"

Jaime smirked. "Nothing, Princess, but I just got paid, so it's my treat. Being short on funds at the end of the month will be Future Jaime's problem."

"I don't want to be the reason you can't pay rent."

"Why don't you just shut up and get in the car? I'm hungry, and the grocery store will be rammed right now, anyway. I swear people start stocking up for Christmas in early October. By this time of the year it's a wild scrum."

"I'll pay you back."

"Nah, you paid last time. Even Stevens." Jaime jingled their car keys. "Come with or I'm going by myself, Wren."

"Alright, alright. At least let me change my clothes first, I feel disgusting from work."

"You mean mopping slush off the floors doesn't make you feel like a pampered regent?"

"Shockingly, no." Wren walked into her bedroom, leaving the door open so they could talk. "I did see an out-of-towner today, though."

"Not that surprising, this close to Christmas. It might be a few weeks out but you know, people travel early to beat the rush."

"No, she's here scouting land and space for a store or something. And then she bought a shop-vac for her friend."

Jaime snorted. "If you ever buy me a shop-vac for Christmas, I'm changing the locks on your ass."

"If I ever have three hundred dollars to spend on you for Christmas, maybe I'll buy you a stack of lottery tickets, help make that dream come true."

"Nah, I'd just let you pay my student loan bill."

"Winning a lottery of a different kind, I guess," Wren replied, taking a fluffy cabled sweater off a hanger. "Sometimes putting on clothes other than my work uniform feels illegal."

"I know what you mean. I put on a pair of jeans today and I thought my manager might show up at the door to arrest me for not complying with the dress code."

"Is she still giving you hell?"

"You know it. Doesn't help that we're slammed as hell with the holiday rush and she flat out refuses to hire anyone else. I went for six solid hours today with no break."

"No wonder you're hangry."

"Yeah, and getting hangrier by the minute. Are you almost done?"

Wren pulled her fleece-lined leggings on under her dark green circle skirt. "Yes, just let me fix my hair."

"Come on, Wren, it's just the diner. It's not a five-star restaurant."

"I know, but we never go out! Sue me for trying to look cute for once."

"I damn well will sue you if I pass out from hunger on the way there. Hurry up, you look fine already. You're an adorable elven being who looks perfect even when you're disheveled. You are a bright, glowing sunbeam on a foggy morning, a crisp breath of fresh air—"

"Okay, fine, let's go," Wren said with a giggle. "Anything to get you to shut up."

"Look at you, the picture of festive adorableness. If you were my type, I would sweep you off your feet and marry you right now."

"You know it would never work, Jaime."

"You're right. We would kill each other. Besides, I have no interest in the fairer sex. I am doomed."

"Come on, you sack of sadness, if we hurry we might get one of the last slices of pie."

"If we don't, it will be your fault for spending three hours preening in front of the mirror like a self-obsessed parakeet."

"It was five minutes and you know it." Wren shoved her feet back into the heavy winter boots, lined with years-old fleece. "Let's go, Chauffeur, chop-chop. I have a garden wrap with my name on it."

* * *

"Two slices of pie, the last ones," their waitress said with a smile, sliding two plates across the table.

"Good thing you didn't decide to curl your hair before we left, then, isn't it?" Jaime asked, a smug tone to their voice as the waitress walked away.

"Yeah, yeah. At least we got them. Looks like pear, apple, cranberry tonight."

"Your favorite?"

"My favorite," Wren confirmed, breaking off a piece with her fork. "This was nice. We don't go out enough."

"Yeah, because we're perpetually broke."

"I appreciate it anyway."

Jaime wolfed down their pie in two enormous bites. "It will change for us one day. I have a good feeling about that."

"Oh, yeah? And what will that look like, exactly?"

"You with your bakery, in that old burger place on Main, employing me as your manager."

"Why would I give you a job as *my* manager?"

"I'm better at marketing than you. You'll make the food, I'll sit in the back room scrolling through social media and taste testing the merchandise. I'll *even* design your logo. Might as well put that design degree to use."

"Sounds like a sweet gig for you."

"I know, doesn't it? I really want that for you."

Wren took another forkful of pie, savoring the spiced sweetness in her mouth. Cinnamon, nutmeg, and the lightest touch of cardamom with the tartness of the cranberries tasted like Christmas. Too bad it would be another lean year for them. "If I'm ever able to open that bakery, I promise with my entire heart to at least consider your application."

"If you don't hire me, I'll burn down your bakery."

"If you burn down my bakery, I will personally drown every plushie you own."

Jaime gave a mock gasp. "You *wouldn't*."

"Say goodbye to Mr. Snuffles, chump."

"Hurry up and finish your pie. I need to drop some stuff at the library before we go home."

"Some of us like to savor our food, alright? It's not my fault you inhaled yours without even tasting it." Wren took another tiny bite, so small it was almost a crumb, just to prove a point.

The door of the diner let in an icy blast and a lone patron.

"Jaime!" Wren hissed. "It's that woman from the store!"

"Why are you whispering?" The woman turned towards them, taking off her tailored pea coat. "Oh, I get it. She's your type. Why didn't you say so?"

"She's not my type, I don't have a type."

"Please, every woman you've fallen madly in love with has the same look."

"What *look*?"

"You know, that tortured, *I have a painful past and I'm emotionally unavailable* look."

Wren scoffed. "That's not true!"

"Sure it isn't. We'll take a stroll through your social media later, shall we? Give me the chance to prove my point?"

"Anyway, Jaime, it doesn't matter, because she's only passing through for a few weeks."

"Interesting that you're *so* disinterested in her that you kept a conversation going long enough to discern that."

"Polite conversation is part of my job."

"I've seen you at your job. You're ninety percent robot."

"A polite robot."

Jaime shook their fork at her. "You *like* her."

"I don't even know her!"

"Don't look now, but she's headed this way."

Wren's stomach flipped, and heat crept up her neck.

"So, you're the one who got the last of the pie," the woman said.

"I, uh... yeah. Sorry. They sell out early. Are you... enjoying the shop-vac?"

"I didn't give it to my friend yet, it's a Christmas gift."

Jaime leaned over the table. "Hi, I'm Jaime, and this is Wren."

"Monroe," the woman said. "And I saw Wren's name tag earlier. I mean, I noticed it. At the shop. It was on the front of her apron."

"I just remembered, I have that thing," Jaime said, gathering their things.

Wren grabbed their arm across the table. "Thing? What thing? You don't have a thing!"

"Yeah, you know, that thing. Call me if you need a ride home, okay? I'll grab the bill at the front."

Jaime, Wren mouthed, but they were already out of the booth, grinning over their shoulder. "Hi," she said aloud.

"Hi." Monroe slid into the booth. "Friend of yours?"

"Yes. My roommate. We share a place on the other side of town. They wanted... pie."

"I don't blame them, I saw the reviews online, this place has quite the following."

"Roberta has loyal fans." Wren pushed the plate across the table. "I feel bad I got the last slice, you should at least try it."

"No, no, I couldn't," Monroe protested. "My own fault for taking too long to decide where to eat."

"Not much of a decision I wouldn't think, there aren't many options in this town."

"I thought about driving back towards the city."

"That's hours away!"

Monroe shrugged. "I like driving. It's relaxing."

"Not for me. I hate it. If I could get away with never sitting behind the wheel, I would. Too many bad drivers around, people who think piloting a one ton piece of machinery makes them a god." Wren bit her lip. "I bet you're not like that, though."

"I try not to let it go to my head."

"I prefer to bike everywhere, but that's hard in the winter here. Too much snow and ice."

"I don't think I've ridden a bike since I was a kid." Monroe leaned back, her elbows resting on the table. "It was fun, from what I remember."

"I really think you should have some pie."

"Normally I'd refuse but... the pie looks *really* good."

Wren pushed the pie further across the table. "It's excellent, and just what you need on a dark and depressing evening like this."

"I like the dark of winter. It's more... private, somehow. Peaceful. Calm." Monroe picked up the fork and took a demure bite. "That's fantastic."

"Finish it."

"Oh, no, you should—"

Wren put her hand up. "I can get this pie whenever I want, assuming I don't take too long to get up here. You're only here a few weeks, you should get your fill."

"If you insist." Monroe took another bite, bigger this time. "I'm sorry, I didn't mean to interrupt your evening. I just don't know anyone here, and... well, you know."

"It can be lonely in the winter."

"Yes, it can."

"Do you ever get sick of travel?" Wren asked. "Ever dream of putting down roots somewhere?"

"That's hard for people like me."

"Why is that?"

Monroe looked up from the pie. "It's complicated."

"Let me guess, estranged from family?"

"Something like that."

"Join the club, then. Jaime and I have both been on our own since eighteen, but we didn't meet until we were both twenty-five."

"Are you...?" Monroe trailed off.

"With Jaime?" Wren laughed. "No. Just friends."

"That's good."

Wren nearly choked on her lukewarm coffee.

"I just mean, maybe you could come by sometime, I'll make you dinner." Monroe smirked. "That's a lie, I can't cook. But I'll order in something. As a thank you for your help earlier."

"I was just doing my job."

"Where else would I find a shop-vac at such short notice?"

"Any hardware store across the country, if I had to guess?" Wren said. "But it's appreciated, anyway. Mr. Ranelli practically climbed the walls with joy."

"Over one sale?"

"It's been... a tough few years for some of the shops here. It can be hard to find reliable work, especially when those huge superstores keep getting built."

Monroe pulled at an elastic band around her wrist. "You deserve better than that."

"Anger management?" Wren asked, nodding at the band. The last thing she needed was to get too friendly with someone who had a habit of punching holes in walls.

"No. Anxiety."

"Do I make you nervous?"

"Yes. But that always happens with beautiful women." Monroe scrawled across the bottom of a clean napkin in green pen and slid it across the table. "The bottom number is my cell, if you decide to take me up on dinner." She smiled again and stood, buttoning up her coat.

As she walked out, Wren folded the napkin into her pocket and texted Jaime for a ride home.

Chapter 4

Monroe sat at the desk, snapping the band against her wrist. She shouldn't get distracted, especially not now. It was a cloudy night, heavy with fog that laid over the ground like a foreboding blanket, but the waxing moon shone bright just the same.

She tapped at the keys, checking one slide, and then another. Everything was in order for the new location, except for the signature of the mayor and the city council. That shouldn't be too hard once she showed them the potential for jobs and growth in the town. It's not like Roanoak Falls was up-and-coming.

Her stomach growled angrily. She'd been in such a rush to look suave that she'd left the diner before even ordering. Fool. There was nothing in this rented house to eat, and she hadn't bothered getting groceries, either. Undereating would only make it worse, especially at this time of the month.

Something like raw need rippled in her muscles, an unwelcome yet familiar feeling. The desire to eat, to feed, to… no, enough. She had a job to get done. She had to focus.

Pain and annoyance shot through her when her stomach cramped with hunger. "Alright, alright," she said aloud. "I guess I'll just get a pizza or something." Scrolling through the local directory, she ordered an extra large pan crust with pickles and olives.

Her phone rang, and she slid the green bar to accept the call. "I'm about to send it over, Steve."

"Hurry it up already, will you? Some of us have lives we'd like to get to."

"This town isn't going anywhere overnight, a few hours isn't going to kill the deal."

"I've seen stranger things, Chase. Don't you remember that development slated for building last year, and some damn social media campaign put the brakes on?"

"Of course I remember. Regional was raging about it for weeks."

"Then I shouldn't have to explain to you why the timeliness is of utmost importance."

"You sound distracted, Steve."

"Same old, same old. They want thirty-five new stores onboarded by the end of the year."

Monroe gave a low whistle. "That's ambitious, considering most everything stops between now and midway through January."

"You think that matters? We need to hit the quarterly target, or we're all out a bonus check."

"I hear you, Steve, I hear you. Listen, I'll be heading up to city hall here tomorrow morning. Maybe we can get this thing signed and you can ship me off to whatever place is next on the list."

"It's always nice to know that I can count on you, Monroe, you know that? I'll sure as hell miss you when they move you up. I bet you'll love it down south, all that warm weather, the beaches, the—"

"Can't wait," she interrupted, seeing the delivery driver's lights flash in through the office window. "Let me know if any other changes need to be made before that meeting tomorrow, I'll be in touch."

"Will do. Bring it home for us, Chase."

She ended the call, shoving the phone into her pocket and jumping down the stairs two at a time. "Just a second," she called through the door.

The phone vibrated with a new incoming call, and she looked from the door to the phone and back. "Damn it," Monroe muttered under her breath. Steve again. She sent it to voicemail and wrenched open the door.

"One extra-large—" the delivery boy started to say, when Monroe's cell phone lit up again. "Are you going to get that?"

"No." She thrust a wad of bills at him. "Keep the change."

"But ma'am it's far too much—"

"Thank you for the pizza!" she yelled, a little too loudly, balancing the pizza in one hand, her phone in the other. Slamming the door, she dropped the box on the ground and accepted the call. "Hello?" she all but shouted into the phone.

"It's Steve, I'm calling from my landline."

"What's up, Steve?"

"I was having a look at your projections, and I think we can do better than that, don't you?"

"But corporate said there's a strict hiring cap on these new builds."

"Yeah, sure, of course, but... I don't know, don't you think it would be a more attractive presentation if you... you know, juiced the figures?"

"You mean lie?"

"It's only a lie if you know it's not true."

Monroe picked up the box and her stomach grumbled in anticipation. "Steve, we *do* know it's not true."

"We don't know that for sure though, do we? I mean, corporate might change their mind. They might decide to offer more managerial positions in the future."

"Hmm."

"Listen, I can feel that you're not on board with this, so if it's a problem I can just put Marcie on this instead."

Monroe sighed. "No, don't call Marcie. I told you, I'll bring this one home. I'll add in the hypotheticals."

"Good. I'd hate to see that juicy promotion go to her and not you, Chase. She annoys me. She's good at her job, but she never shuts up."

"Mmhmm." The thick, greasy, delicious scent of the pizza was incredibly distracting. "Anything else, Steve?"

"Yeah. I'd love to see minutes from your meeting tomorrow."

Monroe stifled a groan. "I'm here on my own, I don't have someone to take minutes."

"A real team player would do it themselves."

"You've never asked for notes before. Why now?"

There was an almost ominous silence at the other end of the line. "Protocol. I've never asked you to step to the line on it before, but now that you're up for the regional position..." he trailed off.

"I get it. Don't worry, I'll send minutes over as soon as I get them typed up."

"Have a good night, Chase. Don't work too hard."

* * *

The door of city hall was worn, the white paint cracked and peeling from years of harsh winters. It creaked as Monroe pulled it open and slipped inside, her eyes adjusting to the dim interior after the snow white brightness of outside.

"Good morning," she said to the bored looking receptionist. "I'm here for a meeting with—"

"It's been rescheduled," he replied, not looking up from his book. "Sorry."

"What do you mean, rescheduled? No one informed me. I drove all the way down here for this! When can we be rescheduled?"

"When the new mayor is in office."

"New mayor?"

The receptionist glanced at her over his half-moon eyeglasses. "Yes. The new mayor. If you bothered to pick up a newspaper..." he trailed off, gesturing vaguely at a rack of papers against the wall, "then you would know that our esteemed leader resigned three days ago. As it turns out, he decided on a whim to retire in Tampa."

"Well, how long will that take?"

"The snap election is next week, just before the holidays."

"Next week—I can't wait for that long, I'm supposed to have this completed by then!" The familiar, foreboding itch at the base of her spine began to creep up her vertebrae. "I could lose a promotion."

"That sounds like a *you* problem."

"Isn't there anyone else I could talk to?"

"You could try the city council."

"Great, when can I schedule a meeting with them?" Monroe asked.

He heaved a long, beleaguered sigh, setting down his book and reaching for a large binder. "They meet on Friday of this week, at six in the evening."

"Can you put me on the schedule?"

"There is no schedule. I'd be surprised if even half of them show up, in fact."

"What kind of city are they running here?"

"I'd wager that the *town* they are running isn't usually in need of emergency meetings," he said in a flat tone. "And the municipal budget doesn't allow for salaries, so the city councilors are volunteers."

Monroe gritted her teeth, exhaling through her nose, eyes squinted shut. "Very well, then, I'll be here at six on Friday."

"Goody."

Snapping the elastic band against her wrist, she chewed on her lip as she exited the small building and walked down the ramp that led to the door. She had to get this under control. It was too close to a new cycle for this much aggravation, and had she known this place wouldn't be a slam dunk, she never would have taken it on.

Monroe slid into the driver's seat of the car and angrily stabbed at the ignition button. Fumbling with the radio, she finally got it to connect with her phone, and the speakers began to intone the deep, rising noise of waves on a beach. "Everything is fine," she said aloud. "Today, I am me, and I am human, and I am in control." She repeated this seven or eight times before the rising twinge in her back subsided.

"I'm in control," she said again. "This is fine." She'd have to call Steve and deliver the bad news. No doubt he'd have Marcie on the first flight out of St. Louis to take over. Damn it all to hell and back.

The line rang three times before he picked up. "That was fast, Chase, even for you."

"The meeting got rescheduled."

"Rescheduled? Why?"

"Something about the town mayor retiring three days ago. You'd think someone at head office would have seen that and, I don't know, ironed out the details before sending me all the way out here."

"And I would think that you'd be able to handle the situation." Steve sighed and then grunted. "What kind of two-bit mayor retires on a whim three weeks before Christmas?"

"One that's moving to Tampa, apparently. I don't even know that I blame him, given the weather here."

"Too cold for you, Monroe?"

"Nah."

"So, when are you rescheduled for?" Steve asked.

"The receptionist said the snap election is next week, but—"

"Next week!"

"—But I can meet with the city council on Friday." Steve was rustling papers so loud, the sound hurt her ears. She held the phone at arm's length. "I figure that's not too bad a delay, given what happened last year."

"Will they even have the authorization?"

"Should be enough for an initial contract, I would think. Enough to announce over the holidays, when people will be less likely to oppose."

"Hmm. That's a good thought, actually. Get it all locked up before anyone can stage a protest. We don't need anyone else chaining themselves to a damned tree. The overtime payments for the demolition crew alone took us way over budget on that."

"We've still got this, Steve."

"You just don't want me to call in Marcie."

"Correct."

He paused, considering. "Fine. Friday. But don't go too wild on the expense card, alright?"

"Steve, I think I would actually find it a challenge to go over my allowances here. It's hardly a place with five-star dining and clubs with fifty-dollar covers."

"Take it easy, Chase, I'm just giving you a hard time."

He wasn't, and she knew it. Whatever was left in the expenses budget at the end of the year wound up as a nice bonus for management at that rank. "I'll call you if anything changes, okay?"

"Sure. Fine."

Chapter 5

Wren stomped up the ramp to city hall and threw open the doors. "I need to talk to someone, *now*."

"There are no appointments available today," the receptionist replied. "Try again after the snap election."

"That isn't good enough. My house has no heat!"

"And how are you hoping to remedy that here, Ms...?"

"Jackson. And I'm hoping that you will go and fix the damn gas line."

"I recommend calling your gas company—"

She planted her hands on the front of the desk and leaned in. "You think I didn't do that already? They informed me that this was part of routine maintenance, and that the city council and the mayor were told about this months ago!"

"Oh, uh..." he put down the book he was reading, something about ancient civilizations and aliens, and began shuffling through a stack of unopened letters. "I don't recall seeing anything from them."

"They said it would have been sent out and confirmed three months ago. Near-emergency maintenance, they said."

"There's nothing in the calendar about it, and I don't see any notices here. Perhaps they've made an error."

"Error or not, my house is basically a block of ice."

"I can try to convene the council before Friday, but it's unlikely. Is there anyone you can stay with until then?"

"The gas company said that someone here would be able to give me a voucher for a hotel or something."

The receptionist grimaced. "I'm afraid I don't have authorization over giving out funds, and there's no one here to sign off on it. Maybe if this had happened last week, the mayor could have sorted it out, but…"

"He's on his way to Tampa already. I know. I read the paper." She sighed, stepping back from the desk. "Isn't there anything you can do for me?"

"The best I can offer is that you keep your lodging and food receipts, and I can try to push the council to reimburse you."

"That's… unfortunately, that's not very helpful."

"If you leave your name and number, I can call the councilors and see if there is anything immediate we can accomplish. However, I have to be honest with you, they are rarely prompt, especially this close to the holidays."

Wren blinked back tears. "Sure." She scribbled her name and phone number on a slip of paper and slid it across the desk. "Thanks."

"I do apologize, Ms. Jackson. Maybe your landlord could—"

"He's out of town until the end of January. I tried."

"I'll call if anything changes."

She turned and pushed the door open, the tears spilling out onto her cheeks. Her phone buzzed with a text from Jaime.

Anything?

No, she typed out in response. *Bastards, all of them.*

"Hey, you okay?"

Wren looked up, shielding her eyes from the sun and her face from view. "Monroe! What are you doing here?"

"I was supposed to have a meeting. It was canceled."

"That seems to be the theme of today."

Monroe leaned back onto the hood of her car, her long hair pulled back into a sleek bun. "I didn't realize you had a meeting here today, too."

"I didn't. The… the effing gas company sliced through my gas line. Apparently, the city council cleared it months ago but never informed me!"

"Is the whole street out?"

"We're a dead end, so it's just us and the place across the street, but it's vacant. New owners aren't moving in until the new year."

"You and Jaime?"

"Yeah."

"Come stay with me. There's more than enough space. I haven't even used the bedroom on the first floor, and I think the sofa is a pull out."

Wren blinked. "What? No, I couldn't impose like that. You barely know us."

"I know I don't want to see you freeze to death. Cold snap is coming in tonight, and snow later in the week." Monroe smoothed her hair back, despite the lack of even a single stray. "Unless you already have somewhere to stay. Friends, maybe?"

"Jaime is kind of it in the friend department since the rest of us moved out of town over the past few years." Wren fumbled with the phone in her pocket, her frozen fingertips sliding over the glassy screen. Jaime couldn't deal with living without heat. Their asthma would be too bad. "Let me ask them."

"Take your time, I don't have anywhere to be."

That Monroe woman from the diner said we can crash at her place, the one she's renting, Wren typed out, hesitating over the next part. *I don't think it's safe or healthy for you to be in the cold for that long, so...*

She sent the message, waiting for a reply. Jaime was never far from their phone.

I hope she's not a cannibal, but if she is, at least we'll die warm, was the response.

"You're not a murderer, are you?" Wren asked casually, leaning over the railing. "Because if you are, we'd at least appreciate a heads-up."

"Of course I'm not a murderer," Monroe shot back, a barbed edge to her tone. "What would give you that impression?"

"Oh, no, it's just... Jaime and I have a weird sense of humor. I know you're not a murderer. This is just an incredibly awkward situation that I really wish I wasn't in."

"Right. Sorry, I work with some intense people."

"I can imagine."

Monroe stepped to the side of the car and opened the passenger door. "Your chariot awaits, then." She checked her watch. "If we hurry, I bet we can still grab lunch. There's nothing at the house, I'm afraid." Before Wren could protest, she offered a wide smile. "My treat."

* * *

"Jaime, over here," Wren said, waving them down. "I ordered your usual."

"I hope you didn't forget the extra pickles," they said, sliding into the booth.

"Of course I didn't. I have met you once or twice."

Monroe set the paper menu down and folded her hands on the table. "Nice to meet you again."

"Yes, it seems you're our guardian spirit, just in time for a made-for-tv movie script," Jaime replied, unbuttoning their thick parka. "Thank you. I don't know why you'd go out of your way for strangers like this."

"I don't know, tis the season, and all that. Besides, I'm in no mood to be visited by three ghosts in the middle of the night. I have a hard enough time sleeping as it is."

"Fair point. Pragmatic, I like it. Wren, what are you getting?"

Wren took a sip of her coffee, blowing at the tendrils of steam that reached up towards the ceiling. "Vegan meatball on ciabatta with extra sauce. I'll give you a bite, but that's it."

"Cheapskate."

"You get extra pickles, so I won't want any of yours, don't even start with me," she said with a laugh.

"Pickles can make or break a sandwich," Monroe said. "Good pickles can transform a mediocre sandwich into a great one. Bad pickles, well..."

"I've never had a pickle I didn't like," Jaime countered. "All pickles are good pickles."

"You never had my grandfather's. Bland, mushy. The man was terrible at pickling, but oh, how he tried. I choked them down just so I wouldn't make him feel bad."

"You were close?"

"For a while. We moved around a lot when I was a kid."

"Military?"

Monroe glanced out the window. "No," was all she said.

"You know, the lighting ceremony is tonight," Wren offered, trying to ease the tension that had settled over the table. "We could go, if you both want. It might be fun?"

Jaime groaned. "It's so pedestrian, Wren. You drag me every year. It's going to be as cold as hell tonight, too."

"I'll go," Monroe said. "I never got to do stuff like that as a kid. My parents weren't into it." She flagged down the server. "More coffee, please?"

The server arched an eyebrow. "You're going to make me think I've got my decaf and caf pots switched. This is your third cup in twenty minutes." She poured more into the stoneware mug on the table.

"I just like caffeine."

"Sure thing, Darlin'."

Monroe took a sip. "Anyway, Jaime, I think there was a spare key at the house you can stay in if you don't want to tag along. There's no food in the fridge, though, so I'll have to get some groceries. Are you allergic to anything?"

"Nothing you'd find in a fridge," Jaime replied. "That's... very nice of you."

"Doesn't everyone always rave about small-town hospitality?"

"Sure, but it's not usually the visitors performing it."

The door of the deli swung wide, letting an arctic blast swoop in around their legs. Wren pulled her sweater tighter around her, hunching over the steaming coffee in front of her.

"Wren, darling, I didn't expect to see you here!" Amber called, brushing the fresh snow off her shoulders. "What an absolute delight. I thought you were working today?"

"Oh, uh... no, Mr. Ranelli gave me the day off."

Amber glanced over at them and frowned lightly before continuing. "Wren, I hope to see you at the campaign launch on Friday?"

"I'm not sure yet, things have gone a little sideways."

"Sideways? How is that?" Amber snapped her fingers at the server. "I shouldn't have to ask for a menu. I always make an effort to shop local, but it's not hard to see why small businesses are failing, is it?"

"Our gas line was cut. No heat until it's fixed."

"You need to go to city hall, Wren. They'll help sort out this mess."

"I was already there. They won't do anything. The receptionist said he'd try to call an emergency meeting, but no guarantees."

Amber rested a hand on her hip. "Well, that would never happen if I was mayor, I can promise you that. Come stay with me, I have plenty of room."

"What about your kids?"

"I doubt they'll even notice you're there."

"We're staying with Monroe, actually," Jaime interrupted. "She was nice enough to offer both of us a place to stay."

"Well, I'm not the local hotel, am I?" Amber huffed. "Besides, I don't even know you. Have we met?"

"I interviewed to be your campaign manager."

"Oh."

"You said I didn't have enough field experience."

Amber turned to Monroe. "I'm sorry, I don't think we've met. I'm Amber Pennington, mayoral candidate. Are you just passing through, or...?"

"I'm here looking to lock down some land for a store expansion, actually," Monroe said, leaning away from Amber. "I ran into Wren at city hall, I was already there for a meeting, but with the mayor's resignation, it has been postponed."

"What kind of store?"

"Oh a... kind of general store, I suppose."

"You can give me your proposal, I can all but guarantee you that I'll be the new mayor in just a couple of short weeks. I've been PTA president at the local school for ten years, there's no way anyone would dare oppose me."

"What a shame," Jaime said, fork poised in their hand. "I love a bit of competition, don't you, Wren?"

"Er, I guess," Wren mumbled.

Amber scowled at Jaime. "I just want whoever is best for the job to have the position." She turned to Monroe with a wide, welcoming smile. "I can't wait to work with you on bringing more business to Roanoak Falls. What company did you say you were with, again?"

"S—actually, I didn't. You probably haven't heard of them. In any case, I'm supposed to meet with the city council on Friday evening to discuss—"

"Friday evening? That can't be. That's when my campaign launch party is!"

"I don't know, Mrs. Pennington—"

"Amber."

"I don't know," Monroe continued, "that's just what the receptionist told me."

"Well, that can't be correct. They really should be waiting for the new mayor to make any major decisions. If you give me your card, I'll give you a ring later with some updated details."

"Oh, I, uh... forgot them."

Amber blinked. "Right. Here's mine, then, don't be afraid to give me a call. I'm sure once they come to their senses, they will reschedule."

The server tapped on Amber's arm. "Ma'am, that menu you asked for."

"Don't you know that it's incredibly rude to interrupt people? My God, the audacity of people."

"Sorry, but it's the lunch rush, and we're short-staffed."

"That's no excuse for poor service, now is it?" Amber snatched at the menu and turned back towards the table. "I've always said you have to demand respect from people, because no one gives it out willingly."

"I've just remembered, I have a conference call in twenty minutes," Monroe announced. "Wren, do you want a ride back? Jaime?"

"I drove," Jaime replied, "but I have to drop by work to pick up my paycheck." They slid out of the booth, tossing a scarf artfully over their shoulder. "I'll catch you both later."

Wren scrambled to wrap up her sandwich in the foil, setting it delicately inside her tote bag. "I'd love a ride, thank you."

As she gave Amber an awkward smile, she noticed Monroe leaving what most would consider a huge tip tucked under a clean water glass. "I'll see you around," she said to Amber.

"At the party on Friday?"

"Maybe!"

Chapter 6

Main Street was packed with people waiting for the lighting ceremony, and Monroe had to weave her way in and out of people, trying not to lose sight of Wren in the crowd. Being in the presence of so many people stressed her out, especially as she'd spent most of her life trying to avoid them. To be alone was to be safe.

"Come on," Wren said over her shoulder, her broad smile beaming brighter than any Christmas lights. "There's a food stand up ahead that's amazing!"

Monroe's stomach growled at the mention of dinner. She was always hungrier when the moon was this bright, and she'd barely eaten her lunch, she was so nervous about the two of them coming to stay with her. What if something happened? She never should have invited them to stay, but the words had tumbled out of her mouth without thinking, and she couldn't take back the offer now.

Her head was already throbbing at the temples, a signal that she needed to eat, and soon. She was swallowing back the sharp irritation that not eating brought. It was both uncomfortable and dangerous. "Food sounds good," she shouted over the din of the onlookers.

"The ceremony will start soon, and then the festival is open to everyone. We could even walk through the gardens, if you want. The lights are beautiful, if you like that sort of thing."

"I'm just following your lead, you're the expert!" The scent of fried fat filled her senses, and she was gripped with pangs from her stomach. "Whatever that is, it smells amazing."

"Corndogs at the stand on the left, and funnel cakes at the stand on the right. Which one do you want?"

"Both."

"A woman after my own heart," Wren said playfully, and then blushed. "Or, you know what I mean." She reached for her bag, but Monroe stepped in front of her.

"It's on me."

"I can't let you do that. You already paid for lunch, and groceries, and you're letting us stay for free!"

"Honestly, it's no problem."

"And I saw that tip you left at lunch."

Monroe turned away; it was her turn to blush now. "I used to work as a server. Some days were hell."

"Mrs. Pennington—Amber—can be a little intense."

"That probably isn't the word I would use, but yes. I work with plenty of people exactly like her."

"I recommend the honey corndog, it's my favorite. I know it sounds weird, but—"

"Excuse me, can we please have four honey corndogs?" Monroe asked the kiosk employee.

"*Four?*" Wren said, astonished.

"I'm hungry, and we should take one to Jaime. They might want one even if they didn't come."

The man in the kiosk grimaced. "I'm sorry, ma'am, we aren't supposed to serve any food until after the ceremony."

Wren laughed. "Since when? It's a light festival, it's hardly a formal affair."

"Some lady came through, she's apparently the committee head for vendors. Amber somebody. She said no food until after so people wouldn't be distracted."

"What if I pay double?" Monroe interjected, her hunger biting into her stomach now. "Triple?"

He shook his head. "I'm real sorry. This is one of our most lucrative events this time of year. We can't afford to get shut down."

"Sure, I understand. Thanks anyway."

"Shouldn't be long now, at least." He closed the window of the kiosk and turned back to the small counter behind him.

"Damn," Wren said. "I'm sorry, I didn't know."

"Don't apologize, it's not your fault." Monroe flinched. Her blood sugar was low, and the itch at the base of her spine was already crawling along every nerve in her body. "Is there something close by, maybe? I hate to miss the ceremony, but I get a little wild when I'm hungry."

"Everything along Main Street will be closed for the night with the festival. If we head back to the car though, there's a place about a mile or so up the road?"

"Do you mind? I'm sorry, I feel like I'm ruining your fun."

"Honestly, the fun is in the craft fair, the garden, the ambiance... the ceremony isn't that exciting. Come on, let's go get something to eat."

Every muscle in her body was tensing. She probably only had twenty minutes before things went south. She should have realized it was too close to the new cycle for this, but... but she had wanted to spend some time with Wren. She was beautiful in that effortless cottage way, in her cute oversized sweaters and patterned leggings, the slightly messy braid—a stab of hunger brought her back to reality.

"Shit, someone blocked the car in," Wren said, craning her neck to look around. "What kind of half-toasted, soggy-ass muffin parks like this?"

"One who couldn't find a parking space." Monroe popped the trunk, silently praying she'd left at least a granola bar in there. She rifled through the half-empty grocery bag, but only found three bottles of sparkling water and a coupon for a local bar-be-cue place. The painful irony. "Damn."

"Are you going to be alright?"

Monroe's eyes were squeezed shut, trying to weather the storm of muscle cramps in her legs without outwardly flinching. "I just don't like being hungry. Low blood sugar, you know."

"I'm sorry, all I have in my bag are breath mints."

"Are there bathrooms around here, do you know?"

"Sure, over there near the office block across the street, those won't have a line. The ones closer up by Main Street will."

"I'll be right back, okay?"

Wren's brow furrowed. "Okay."

It was her worst nightmare. She'd taken so many precautions in her life, but one day of slip-ups and everything was falling apart. It was already starting, she could feel her bones begin to shift under her skin. It would be unnoticeable to others, at first. People didn't tend to notice until the final change began.

Monroe slipped past the bathrooms behind the office building, hoping against hope for a small, tree-lined thicket, or at least an empty lot with a dumpster to hide in, or—

She stopped in her tracks and quietly ducked under the half-open warehouse door. This would have to do. If she could just concentrate, maybe she could fight it, beat it back until she could get somewhere safe.

Monroe groaned, bent double and holding her stomach. It was always so painful. She resented every muscular deviation, the slow, torturous process of becoming a monster. A beast. It had been almost a year since the last time, and every follicle of fur that pushed up through her skin was like a tiny bayonet. Tears welled in her eyes and fell, but that was no surprise. They splashed onto the concrete as she fell on all fours. It would happen fast, now.

She tossed her coat and blazer aside, along with her shoes, every movement a trial. It took every ounce of self-control to not scream through the pain, to give in to the feral danger that threatened to spill out of her. Another wave of bones breaking and reforming inside her skin and she bit back a cry of terror. Once it happened, she was vulnerable. Alone. If someone found her... people in the Midwest were unlikely to be kind to a monster.

The warehouse was mercifully empty, except for a small forklift on the far end and boxes of files stacked neatly nearby. If anyone was working late, she'd be in trouble. She scanned the ceiling for telltale red lights, relieved when she found none. Being caught on camera would be the end of her life as she knew it.

The rest of the clothes she wore tore, the seams straining, the buttons of her shirt popping, flying through the air, rolling along the cracked concrete before coming to a rest, strewn across the warehouse. She backed into the corner, pressing her flesh against the railing that bit into her despite the thick fur.

"Monroe?" Wren called from the alley outside.

No, not now. Not here. Fear enveloped her, swallowing her whole until she was drowning in adrenaline and a toxic cocktail of nervous responses. Bile spewed from her mouth, a sickly green foam and nothing else. It was her own fault for neglecting to eat. She knew better.

"Monroe, are you in here? The lighting is about to start." Wren's boots crunched over the newly fallen snow, already crusted into ice in the cold. "I can call Jaime to pick us up if you're not feeling well. Your car is still blocked in, and I can't find the chucklehead who parked there."

Maybe if she was so quiet, and so still, she would be left alone. The railing pressed further into her skin as she pushed herself as far back as she could go, and groaned softly from the pain.

Wren glanced towards the half-open door. "Are you in here?" She bent, squinting into the darkness. "Who's there?"

The warehouse door's motion sensor light clicked on, flooding them both in garish yellow light.

"Holy—what the—" Wren stumbled backwards, slipping on the ice.

Monroe tried to hide her face from the light, turning back to the shadows, scraping against the metal stairs in a futile bid to escape. Didn't Wren know that she was dangerous? A monster? That she could easily kill her with one swipe?

Footsteps echoed across the empty loading bay. No doubt Wren was running to get help, to tell everyone that a bear was in the warehouse. More fear, clouding her sight and obscuring her memories. Had she even been Monroe at all? Maybe she'd always been like this.

When she turned, Wren was gone.

It was for the best. At least she couldn't hurt her now. Hunger tore at her, made her feel out of control. She pawed through boxes, desperate for food. There was nothing. The shelves were bare, holding few boxes this time of the season, as offices were winding down for the year. Not that it would have mattered - it was an office building and a warehouse full of paperwork, not a storeroom full of nourishment.

She was nothing except fear and hunger, nothing but wild impulses that overtook anything like sense or reason. Fighting against the fog, she struggled with choice. Stay in the warehouse and wait for this to pass, hopefully by morning? Or find her way out, risk trying to find somewhere safe? Even if she did, she'd have no clothes, and there were too many people to get to the car once she returned to her normal form. The sound of footsteps in the alley sent a fresh wave of roiling acid washing through her empty belly. They were coming.

"I brought you something," Wren said from the doorway, with an armful of corndogs. "I used the cash from the glove box in the car."

Monroe sat back on her haunches.

"I am scared, so I'm going to put these down here for you and wait outside." Wren began to remove the sticks from the corndogs. "I didn't tell anyone." She piled the food into a messy pyramid and backed out of the warehouse, watching cautiously from the other side of the door.

The smell was intoxicating. It was like nothing she'd ever smelled before, hot, fried, salty, with a touch of sweetness that made Monroe's mouth water. She shoved her face into the pile, devouring them two, three at a time until nothing but crumbs were left.

Wren peeked under the door. "Are you done?" She eased back inside, holding her arms out in front of her. "I really hope I'm not losing my marbles. Please don't eat me." She approached, slowly. "If you do eat me, I don't blame you, but please don't."

Her eyes squeezed shut. Monroe only felt fear, even from Wren. All she wanted was to be left alone to wallow, to rot like the diseased garbage that she was, unlovable, unwanted. She felt a hand on her face and flinched away.

"Hey, it's okay." Wren laid her other hand on Monroe as well, and knelt down in front of her. "See? Safe. Everyone is watching the lighting. No one is coming back here."

The fear, shame, and guilt melted away. Monroe laid her face on Wren's shoulder and her heart rate finally slowed back to normal, all at once desperately grateful and relieved. No one was coming for her. Tomorrow would be a new day.

"I'm going to stay here until you don't want me to," Wren said, shivering in the cold.

Monroe curled around her, the exhaustion dragging at her eyelids. She couldn't sleep. Not yet. Another hour passed, with Wren whispering reassurances on occasion. The moon was high in the sky now, the cold white beams gleaming on the frosted snowbank outside.

After a while, the shift began to fade, her bones returning to their rightful place, her skin now raised from the freezing temperatures. When she was able to speak, she only said, "I have spare clothes in the car."

Wren left, and returned with a duffle bag stuffed with sweatpants, a hoodie, and underthings. As Monroe dressed, she faced the wall, despite the fact Wren had already seen everything. The more human she became, the more embarrassed she felt.

"I put your clothes in the bag," Wren said. "I don't think we'll be able to clean up this warehouse, though."

"No."

"Do you want me to drive us home?"

Monroe nodded. "Yes."

The midnight air was cold enough to take their breath away, the icy tendrils reaching down into their lungs. The car didn't take long to heat up, and they both held their frozen fingers in front of the vent.

"Did you at least eat one of those corndogs?" Monroe finally asked.

"No. You owe me one."

"I owe you a lot more than that."

Wren stared out the windshield, her hands on the steering wheel now. "Is that... normal, for you?"

"Since I was eleven."

"Are there others?"

"I don't think so."

"Does it hurt?"

Monroe blinked back tears. "Terribly." She wiped her cheeks with the sleeve of her hoodie. "How did you know it was me?"

"I just knew." Wren put the car into reverse, pulling out of the small parking lot. "I was worried when you ran off, I thought you might pass out or something. I didn't expect... that."

"I'm sorry."

"You should have told me."

"Would you have believed me?"

Wren sighed. "No. Probably not." She turned onto the dark country highway, the high beams on. "I lied to Jaime. I told them we went out to a bar."

"Did they buy it?"

"I don't think so, they always know if I'm lying. But for now, it's okay."

"Did I scare you?" Monroe asked.

"I'm glad you didn't eat me."

"To my knowledge I've never eaten a human."

"To your *knowledge*?"

"Sometimes it gets a little hazy."

Wren flicked the radio on, the volume low. "I just need something normal."

"I understand."

"Are you still hungry? Do you need something else to eat?"

"Yes. But I can make something at the house."

"I have a better idea."

Chapter 7

Wren's hands were still shaking as she unpacked the six rotisserie chickens from the bags and lined them up on the granite countertop, but she steeled herself and smiled anyway. "Ready to eat?"

"Hell yes," Monroe replied, putting a whole chicken on her plate alongside an enormous portion of seasoned potato wedges. "This was better than anything I'd have cooked up here." She tore off a leg and took a bite. "I'm not much of a chef."

"Me neither. I prefer baking," Wren replied, slicing off a few pieces for herself. "I enjoy the quiet precision of a loaf of bread."

"I tried to bake a few times, you know, using boxes from the store. Never worked out as well as I wanted them to."

"I can teach you a few tricks to liven them up, if you want. Personally, I think everything tastes better with extra chocolate."

"Agreed." Monroe picked one chicken clean and started on another. "I'm sorry," she said before taking another bite. "For all this."

"Did you know that would happen?"

"No. I mean, it's always a possibility, never something I welcome."

"So you don't have control over it?"

"No."

"At all?" Wren asked.

"I do my best to keep it at bay. My parents had me see every specialist in the country. None of them believed it until they saw it. Most wanted to report me, but my parents paid them handsomely to keep quiet."

"What causes it?"

Monroe dipped three wedges at once into some ranch dressing. "No one knows. Could be anything, a genetic mutation, maybe. I just know that I hate everything about it."

"It must have been terrifying for you."

"Still is."

"No, I mean, when you were a kid."

"Is it okay if we don't talk about that?"

Wren nodded. "Of course. It's just... a lot. To take in."

"I know. I thought you'd run screaming to the nearest festival security guard and turn me in. Not many bears in Roanoak Falls, I imagine."

"None that I'm aware of, no. At least, not since I've lived here."

"And how long has that been?"

"A while now. Left home at eighteen. Spent a few years in the city, but I hated it. Loud, expensive, frenetic. I was a mess. Decided to start over somewhere quieter. Wound up here, met Jaime, the rest is history, I guess."

"Do you like it here?"

Wren thought for a moment, picking at her chicken. "I do. I wish some things were different."

"Like what?"

"I wish Main Street was more vibrant. It's been dulled down by franchises and chains, big corporate players who don't give a rat's ass about the town or the people who live in it. I just imagine how different things could be, if we decided as a town to prioritize small businesses, if we had artist spaces and a city hall that didn't look like it was one strong wind away from blowing over."

"Sounds like you should be the one running for mayor, not Amber Pennington."

"I would hate it, being tied to that kind of daily structure. My dream is to be left alone in a kitchen to create cakes and pastries."

"Idyllic," Monroe agreed, starting on another chicken.

"What's your dream? Or is this what you love, scouting out new places for stores? What store was it, again?"

"It's..." Monroe trailed off. "I don't know, actually. I spent so long searching for a cure that I forgot anything else existed. It's a job, it pays well. Very well, in fact, but if you're asking me what gets me out of bed in the morning... I couldn't tell you. Maybe it's the constant search for something better out there."

"Did you ever get close to finding a cure?"

"Never. I've tried everything, from genome sequencing to sensory deprivation tanks and yoga. The best I can do is stave it off as long as I can." Monroe raised her left wrist. "Grounding works, sometimes. Other times it just takes over and all I can do is try to ride it out."

"Do you always eat this much?" Wren put a hand over her mouth, disgusted with herself for even asking the question. "I'm so sorry, that was very rude of me to ask."

Monroe laughed. "It's alright. Yes, after a shift my metabolism kicks into extremely high gear, I spend the next couple days constantly ravenous."

"Will it happen... again?"

"It's hard to say. Probably not, it's more or less aligned with lunar cycles, but it's happened." She looked up from the half-eaten chicken. "I always get sick after."

"Why?"

"You're full of questions, aren't you?"

Wren bit back a frown. "Not to put too fine a point on it, but I just saw a bear turn back into a human. Most people would have questions."

"I know, I'm sorry, it's just... I'm really tired. I'm gonna finish this last chicken and go fall into bed." Monroe crammed the last of the food into her mouth, chewing quickly, and swallowed. "Jaime has the spare key, don't feel like you have to wait for me or anything tomorrow. I'm sure you're busy."

The date with Amber hung heavily on Wren's mind. "Mm," she agreed. "Good night."

* * *

"What the hell happened here last night?" Jaime demanded, staring at the chicken bones with relative horror. "It looks like fifteen people had the munchies."

"Don't worry, no one had a party without you."

"Yeah, no kidding, Wren. I was asleep in the next room. Are you going to tell me what actually happened at the festival, or are you going to make me guess?"

"I don't have time for this, I'm going to be late."

"You... ran into your ex, and she was particularly nasty?"

"No."

"Did you get drunk at a bar and get a craving for... six chickens?"

Wren laughed. "No."

"True, you've never been a big drinker. Hmm." Jaime filled a bowl with sugary cereal and poured milk over the top as they thought. "Did something bad happen? You'd tell me if you were in trouble, right?"

"I'm not in trouble."

"Then what is it?"

"Nothing!" Wren shot back, and already the guilt of the lie was nesting heavily in her stomach. "I told you, we went to the festival, we had some fun, but the lines at the kiosks were too long so we went to a bar for a drink, got food, and came home."

Jaime squinted at her over their bowl of cereal. "If you say so."

"I do say so."

"Did Monroe have fun? Did you see Amber there?"

Wren groaned. "Don't remind me. I'm supposed to go to dinner with her tonight."

"Ew, why?"

"She showed up at work and just kept asking. It's free dinner?"

"Tell her you're sick. Better yet, tell her to go take a hike. She's gross, Wren, she's mean, and petty and you know it."

"She used to be nicer when I was watching her kids. When they were younger."

"Yeah, that was before she decided the only right way to be a human was to step on other people to get what she wanted. She chose the wrong path. Besides, she didn't hire me, so you should automatically hate her, that's the real test of friendship. Me, or some girlboss in a Chanel pantsuit?"

"You're acting like I want to go out with her."

"Don't you?"

Wren's mind was on Monroe in the bedroom upstairs. "Not really." She sighed. "But if she does become mayor, she'll have a say in zoning laws. Might make sense to keep her on our side?"

"Your side, I think you mean. Don't think I don't remember that little crush you had on her."

"Does that mean you're giving up the future job as my marketing manager?"

Jaime gave her a wry smile as they tossed the bowl into the sink and rinsed it. "Very funny, Jackson. Listen to me. If you go to this dinner, make it clear you're not interested. That woman has her sights set on you. Wren Jackson, first lady of Roanoak Falls."

"Shut up," Wren said, throwing a clementine at them. "I don't even know if I'm going. If I have any luck, Mr. Ranelli will make me work closing."

* * *

"No, you can have the night off," Mr. Ranelli said, examining the giant lit reindeer. "Mrs. Pennington came by earlier and said she needed you for something important?"

"Oh, it's nothing," Wren replied casually. "I can totally work closing if you need me to."

"Go on, enjoy yourself. You work too much."

"You're the one who schedules me."

He sighed, repositioning the reindeer so that it was facing the front of the store. "Truth be told, Wren, I'm not so sure how long we can keep this whole thing running. I didn't want to tell you until after Christmas, but..."

"But?" Wren prompted.

"Did you know that Roanoak Falls was tapped as a possible site for a new Syndicorp multi-store?"

"No. How did you find that out?"

"I've lived here my whole life. Long enough to have ears where there shouldn't be, if you catch my drift. All those long lunches I've been taking,

I've been meeting with an old friend in the next county. Word has it they're aiming to break ground in late spring or early summer next year."

"It's not for sure though, right?"

"Nothing is for sure other than death and taxes, but it sure feels inevitable. I've got a feeling Mrs. Pennington will soon be Mayor Pennington, and she's all too keen to corporatize this town in the name of growth. Says there's too many out of work. I don't know, maybe she's right, and it's what's best for this place, but I can't help feeling a little selfish."

"We could still make it work. Send out flyers, maybe, or—"

Mr. Ranelli shook his head. "You know as well as I do that we can't compete with those kinds of prices. No amount of flyers will change that."

Her stomach sank. "So that's it, then? We're just going to give up?"

"I shouldn't have told you." He gave her a weak smile. "This store has been in my family for three generations, you know? I feel like a failure for being the one to close up shop for good."

"It's not your fault."

"Go on, get out of here. Enjoy yourself. Who knows, if Mrs. Pennington winds up as mayor, maybe we can both call in favors. We'll work the home improvement section together, eh?"

Wren chewed the inside of her cheek. "Are you sure you're okay?"

"Fine, just fine. Nothing a cold beer and a sad movie won't fix." He waved at her, gesturing at the door. "Go on, get! I'll see you tomorrow afternoon."

It was colder, if that was even possible. Wren shivered at the bus stop, breathing into her hands to stop the ache in her fingers. It wasn't much better aboard the bus, either, and when she stopped at home to grab some clothes, there was already frost on the inside of the windows. She couldn't even imagine what it would be like if Monroe hadn't offered to let them stay.

Shoving some sweaters and fleece-lined tights into a bag, Wren sighed. *Merry Christmas, you're probably losing your job. Another year, another crappy holiday.* She locked the door behind her and started the walk to her temporary abode, latent snow listing under the orange glow of the streetlights as they flicked on, one by one.

The house was eerily quiet with Jaime at work, and Monroe nowhere to be seen. Wren kicked the snow off her boots and climbed up the stairs two at a time to find herself faced with a closed door, with no signs of movement.

She knocked. "Monroe? Are you in there?" There was no answer, but the sound of shifting bed sheets eked out under the heavy oak door. "I'm going to head out soon. Do you need anything?" Still no answer.

Wren sighed and descended the stairs again, changing out of her work clothes in the downstairs bathroom. What if Monroe was too sick to cook? She had mentioned getting ill after... that. After braiding her hair and pinning it up, she chopped vegetables, carrots and celery, adding the shreds of chicken that were left to the pot.

When Amber pulled in the drive and beeped the horn, Wren left the bowl of soup at Monroe's door. "I made you some chicken noodle," she called. "I'll be back later." She paused for a moment, her hand on the doorknob. "I'm going out with Amber."

Chapter 8

The front door slammed, and Monroe eased her own open, the delicate creak echoing across the hallway. The rich scent of homemade chicken noodle soup wafted up in steamy tendrils from the bowl Wren had left at her door. Something about it made Monroe's chest tight, uncomfortable, and heavy with emotion.

It was just soup. What was the big deal?

Homemade soup, though, and it smelled amazing.

She picked up the bowl, the warmth tingling through her fingers and up into her palms. Sitting on the edge of her bed, she slurped at it. Savory and tempting, she drained the rest of it in just a few gulps, relishing the tender chicken and perfectly cooked noodles.

The house was empty, and she was finally alone to examine her beastly self in the bathroom mirror, her visage even more frightening under the fluorescent light over the sink. There were dark circles under her eyes; to be expected after a night like she'd had. But there were other things, too. A fine dusting of fur across her ribcage. She gasped, turning away from her reflection.

Once a shift was over, she was supposed to return to her full human self. That's what all the specialists had always said, anyway. Her parents had never encouraged abnormal behavior before, during, or after, even limiting her to what they considered a normal portion of food.

Her stomach growled at the memory, reminding her that she was grown now, and they lived thousands of miles away, across an ocean. She could eat whatever and whenever she wanted. Maybe more food would encourage the rest of her to shift back, to erase the last vestiges of the beast she'd never wanted to become.

Wren had left the rest of the soup on the stove, with a note scrawled in round cursive so neat, it looked like a font.

The rest is for you. We'll be back later. Text if you need anything.

Her cell number was at the bottom. Monroe tapped it into her contacts list, dropping her phone back into the pocket of her sweatpants. She hadn't even changed since last night, the sweat crispy on the back of her collar. She poured out the soup, still hot, and ate it all, bowl by bowl.

She drained half a gallon of orange juice from the fridge, then toasted and ate half a loaf of seeded rye bread with butter and jam before she started to feel better. Her body still ached from the shift, but her head was clearer, at least.

Her phone vibrated against her thigh. Steve. Of course it was going to be Steve.

"Good morning, Chase, I'm just calling to check in?"

"Hi, Steve."

"Any news?"

"No news. Meeting isn't until tomorrow, remember?"

"I'd hoped that maybe you had convinced the city council to convene an emergency meeting... no?"

Monroe stifled a sigh. "I'm afraid not."

"Listen, there's been a change in plans. National wants us to expedite our goals, they want to double the new stores in the same time frame."

"*Double?* But—"

"They're talking a new unit every seven to ten miles."

"The stores would be cannibalizing each other's customer base."

"It still all goes back to corporate," Steve explained. "More dividends are more dividends, no matter how you slice it."

Monroe tapped the edge of the coffee pot. Cold. She switched the phone to her other hand and dumped out the used grounds. "Surely the franchise owners won't like that."

"No, but our contracts are ironclad. We never promised them area exclusivity."

"It's going to kill franchise recruitment stone dead, Steve."

"Good thing franchise recruitment isn't our department then, isn't it? Not our circus, not our clowns, not our problem. Let the VPs deal with it."

"I just can't help but think that this is all going to blow up in our faces. It feels... short-sighted." She dumped fresh grounds into a filter, the rich scent already waking her up. "This isn't about another merger, is it?"

"I couldn't say."

"That's a yes, then. Beef out the number of stores so the bottom line looks thicker than it really is."

"They don't pay us for feedback, Chase. Or to have morals. We're paid to get the job done, collect our paychecks, and get on with it. High ideals don't pay the mortgage."

"No, I know, it's just..." Monroe trailed off, and frowned at the display on the coffee maker. How the hell did this thing turn on? "It's just that I think Syndicorp might have a better reputation in towns like this if they didn't, you know."

"Maximize profits?"

"Screw people over."

"Syndicorp is a job creator, you know that."

"One of the biggest employers in the country, I know."

"You're not going soft on me, are you?"

Monroe rolled her eyes, grateful he couldn't see her. "No, Steve, I'm not *going soft*. I'm just trying to present what a long game would look like if we stay on this path. No one wants years of litigation biting into our bonuses."

"Right you are about that. Do me a favor, just get this one locked down tomorrow, and we'll put our heads together in the new year about the expansion plans."

"Sure thing." She knew that light, dismissive tone from him. It meant he was placating her. He had no intention of raising concerns to management about why this was all a terrible idea. He was just hoping that she'd forget about it, or at least stop bringing it up. "I'll call you after the meeting."

"No news on a potential new mayor?"

"Nothing concrete."

"Hmm." He sucked his teeth. "Shame. Alright, Chase, enjoy the rest of your day. Get those charts prepped."

The line went dead just as the coffee began to brew, and a frigid draft seeped under the front door. She'd have a long night worrying about that meeting. Strong coffee, cream, and sugar, and a thick chenille blanket on the couch while she nursed her aching joints.

* * *

The television gave the room a gentle hum that was better than the cold silence she'd started with. It was already nine in the evening. Why hadn't Wren or Jaime returned yet? Monroe switched the channel, choosing a cooking show instead of the nightly news, even though it would only make her hungry. She'd never been much of a cook, not really, but once, in her twenties, she'd taken a short course at the local college. That was before her job had taken her on the road, though.

She frowned at the laptop, open to a page listing hundreds of bookmarked websites where she'd tried to find a cure. None of them had helped, not even the ones she thought might have been run by other... well, whatever she was. A beast. A monster. Something that was wholly undeserving of love. But there weren't any others, and she was still alone.

All those years spent scraping the internet for answers had come to nothing. Gene therapies as a teenager hadn't helped, nor had hormone treatments, muscle relaxers, or sedatives. The beast within her always showed up, regardless of any precautions. The best she could do was try to keep it at bay.

The potato chips she'd grabbed from the kitchen were pretty good. They didn't have this brand all over, it seemed to be a local thing. The flavors of onion and dill coated her mouth, the saltiness deeply satisfying. She tapped her fingers against the keys, not hard enough for letters to appear in the search bar. What could she even look for that she hadn't thousands of times already? Even the deepest recesses of the largest libraries hadn't held anything for her other than vague references to what were probably nothing more than myths.

"This is stupid," she said aloud with a grunt, and closed the laptop lid. Another chip went into her mouth and she chewed defiantly. "Pointless."

She turned the volume up on the cooking show to drown out the buzzing in the base of her spine. The full moon was still days away, but if she wasn't careful, she could turn again. The host of the show was a stocky, chirpy man with a kind face, the grey hairs peeking out through his thick beard. He was making some sort of lamb dish, it looked like.

Monroe's stomach rumbled again. "I just fed you!" she protested, shoving another chip into her mouth. "And it's not like I can just magic up a rack of lamb."

"When you've finished cleaning up, I want you to take a moment to appreciate what you've accomplished," the man on the television said softly. "You are a bright spark in the world, and you are deserving of love, affection—and this amazing meal. Let's dig in."

The camera panned across the succulent feast as the host cut a section to show the audience at home. "Mm," he said, taking a bite. "That is worthy of you." He put the fork down. "To all of you watching, I want you to spend some time this week to appreciate the way you were made. Embrace who you are."

"Oh, shut up," Monroe said, changing the channel. "Some of us were born monsters. It's hard to embrace that." She jerked at the sound of keys in the door.

"Hey," Wren said, hanging her bag on a hook. "Who were you just talking to?"

"No one. My boss." Monroe held out the bag of chips. "How was your date?" Her stomach turned at the thought. She smiled at Wren through the envy. "Good?"

"Weird."

"Weird how?"

Wren perched at the counter, waiting for the teakettle to whistle. "She's very... persistent? I don't know, maybe that's the wrong word to use. Determined, maybe, but in a way that just feels sort of oppressive."

"Yeah, I know the type."

"She's so convinced that she's going to win the mayoral campaign that she's already talking to property developers. Did you know that?"

Monroe's ears perked up. "Like who?"

"Syndicorp, would you believe it? She's talking left and right about property values and market rents, job creation and how good it will look for a new mayor to have projects in motion right away."

"She spoke to... Syndicorp?"

"I know! After everything this town has been through, when the lumber mill closed down twenty years ago, struggling to keep this place alive, and now she wants to bring in the grim reaper to finish the job."

Monroe narrowed her eyes. Marcie. It had to be.

"What's wrong?" Wren asked.

"Nothing. Just tired." She turned the television off and leaned over the back of the sofa. "Thank you for the soup. It was delicious."

"I see you finished it off. Good. You'll need your strength."

"No one has ever... made soup for me before."

"Not even your mother?"

Monroe snorted. "*Especially* not my mother."

"We're running low on bread. We should get some tomorrow, if you're feeling up to it."

"I hope so." The itch beneath her skin sank deep into her muscles. "I still feel a little weird. I probably will until the moon starts to wane."

"Don't you have a meeting at city hall tomorrow?"

"I do, but not until six."

"You know, I don't work until two. We could get breakfast, if you want."

"I don't know if I'm ready to face people yet," Monroe replied with a grimace. "What if I make you breakfast, instead? As a thank you for the soup?"

"I thought you said you weren't much of a cook."

"I'm not, but if burned scrambled eggs sound appealing, then I can absolutely help you in that arena."

Wren laughed just as the tea kettle began to whistle. "Shockingly, I prefer my eggs unburnt, if you would believe that." She filled a mug with water, the tea bag swimming. "Do you want tea?"

"Sure."

"Are you hungry?"

"Perpetually, apparently." Monroe stood and stretched, her limbs stiff from spending all day in bed. "Did you eat at dinner?"

Wren nodded. "I did, but I could always go for snacks."

Chapter 9

Wren leaned her head against the car window, her breath fogging up the half-frozen glass. She'd barely slept, tossing and turning on the sofa, unable to quiet her noisy thoughts.

"What's eating you?" Jaime asked, braking at a stoplight. "You've barely said a word all morning. You don't work until later this afternoon, yet you shot out of the house this morning like you were late for your own wedding."

"Nothing. I don't know."

"How was your date? You brushed me off last night when I asked."

"Fine."

Jaime glanced over, an eyebrow arched. "Try again, Wren. Something is bugging you, what is it?"

"Have you ever seen something unbelievable?"

"Sure, I once saw a Democrat in a deep red county."

"No, that's not what I mean—I mean something that's so wild and fantastic, you think you might be losing it."

"Are you about to tell me that you've seen God or something? Have you been visited by an angel who wants to teach you the real meaning of Christmas?"

Wren snorted. "No—stop making me laugh! I'm serious!"

"What's going on, Wren? Is this about the other night? What happened?"

"I'm not sure if I should tell you."

"I can keep a secret," Jaime said, their eyes front now as the light changed to green. "I never told anyone that you had that crush on the woman who worked at the diner a couple of years back. You know, the one with the scary clown tattoo."

"This is different."

"Can you at least tell me if you're in danger or not? You're scaring me now. I'm not an anxious person and this is making me feel jittery."

"Sorry. I'm *probably* not in any danger."

"Okay, so you didn't witness a murder, then."

"I said it was wild and fantastical, not grisly and depressing," Wren replied. "It's not anything that someone could be arrested for." She bit her lip. "I don't think."

"Is this about Monroe? She's barely left her room. Is she sick, or something?"

"Or something."

"Is she pregnant?"

Wren gave an exasperated sigh. "What about someone being pregnant is so unbelievable that I'd feel like I was losing it? Stop trying to guess, you're not going to get it."

"I bet I could get it. You don't have to say anything, I'll just say some scenarios and your silence can confirm or deny the truth of it."

"Jaime, I don't think this is a good idea. I—"

"Was it... a royal, disguised as common folk to meet his true love?"

"No."

"A time-traveler, sent to warn you of your fate in Christmases to come?"

"Yes, the time-traveler told me I'd be working Christmas Eve again next year."

Jaime laughed. "Wouldn't take a time-traveler to know that. Okay, was it a lonely reindeer in the forest, looking for Santa's sleigh?"

"If there was a reindeer in the woods around here, someone would have eaten it already."

"True." Jaime drummed their fingers against the steering wheel. "Did a snowperson come to life?"

"While the absolute horror of that would definitely keep me up at night, I'd probably be barricading myself in the house with a flamethrower, not driving around with you."

"Maybe I'm in the wrong season. Vampires?"

"You mean, other than our landlord?"

"Ha! Good one. Ghosts? Zombies? Werewolves?" Wren didn't say anything. Jaime laughed, enjoying the game. "Well, which is it? Zombies?"

"No zombies," Wren said, her voice barely above a whisper. "Or ghosts."

Jaime pulled into the parking lot of the local donut shop. "I sincerely hope this is you committing to the joke."

"Not a wolf."

"But a were?"

She nodded, her face in her hands. "You can't say anything."

"Wren, if we tell anyone that, they'll throw us on a seventy-two hour mandatory psychiatric hold, and I can't do that ever again. Did you do mushrooms or something at the festival?"

"No!"

"No one slipped you anything? Do we need to get you a drug test? If anyone dosed you, I swear I will hunt them down and—"

"No one drugged me. I swear to you, this was *real*."

"Hallucinogens *do* feel real."

"Jaime."

They clasped both their hands on the steering wheel, despite the car being parked and the engine off. "I need you to tell me what happened now, because I have literally never been more worried about you. You know I am worried because I am still sitting here in the car, when fresh donuts are ten steps away."

"You can't tell her I told you."

"I won't tell her."

Wren exhaled slowly, her breath rising to the roof of the car in curl tendrils of smoke. "She turned into a bear."

"A bear."

"Yes."

"And you're telling me that no one else at the lighting ceremony noticed?"

"She hid in the loading bay or whatever of that office building behind Main Street. I... helped her."

"You helped a bear?" Jaime asked, incredulous. "And here I thought you actually had an ounce of self-preservation. A bear, Wren. They eat people."

"She was scared and alone."

"What kind of bear?"

"I don't know, a big one. Mostly brown, with a little grey."

"And you're sure that was her and not some random friendly woodland bear you came across?"

"I saw her change," Wren said slowly. "Back into a human."

"I suppose that explains the rotisserie carnage in the kitchen yesterday."

"She gets hungry after, she said. And sick."

Jaime pulled the keys from the ignition. "I need copious amounts of sugar to deal with this news. You want anything?"

"We should get something for Monroe. Maybe two dozen variety and one of those breakfast sandwiches on a croissant. I want one of those, too." Wren pulled her wallet from the bag at her feet. "She left money on the kitchen counter for breakfast."

"Must be nice to have so much cash in the bank that you can throw money at practical strangers."

"Jaime..."

"I'm not complaining about a free breakfast, Wren. I'm just saying we deserve better than our current bank balance."

* * *

"So, you're a Bear?" Jaime asked, throwing their keys on the counter.

"Jaime, you said you wouldn't tell her!" Wren protested.

"I want to make sure you're not going to get torn to shreds, don't I? Next thing I know they'll find you in the woods, half eaten next to a pile of corndog sticks."

Monroe had frozen mid-sip of coffee, staring at both of them.

"I'm sorry, they figured it out," Wren said. "They won't tell anyone."

"I need to go," Monroe said, setting the full mug on the table and reaching for her coat near the back door. "I need to leave Roanoak Falls, uh... the house

61

is paid up for the next two weeks. Feel free to stay."

"But—"

"Do you know what they'd do to someone like me if the wrong people found out? They'd lock me in a cage in a lab somewhere, they'd hook me up to machines and I'd never see the light of day again. My parents may have managed to keep my medical records sealed, but they had the law on their side, along with several offshore accounts full of cash."

"Wait," Wren said, catching her by the wrist. "Don't leave. We just want to help."

Monroe flinched, but didn't pull her arm away. "You said you wouldn't tell anyone."

"I'm sorry, they knew I was hiding something."

"I always know," Jaime interjected. "It's like a superpower."

"I never should have come here," Monroe said softly. "This... place, it's going to be my undoing. All the work I put into rigidity and predictability, it's... it's all falling apart." She cringed away from some invisible pain. "I don't deal well with confrontation."

Jaime held out a large box of donuts. "No one is confronting you. We even brought a peace offering, see?"

"You literally said you thought I'd leave her half-eaten in the woods."

"I'm a little dramatic, so sue me."

Monroe pulled away now, tears welling in her eyes. "I've never hurt a human, never. I'd never. I have tried too hard to rid myself of this curse and I'm stuck with it, but I'd never hurt anyone, especially Wren."

"I'm sorry, I—"

"Just forget it. I'm going to go pack. I have a meeting tonight. I'll leave town straight from city hall. Merry Christmas, or whatever."

"Monroe, wait, please don't go," Wren asked. "Please. I'm sorry, truly, we just... you've done so much for us already, we want to try to pay you back."

"You can pay me back by never mentioning this to anyone, ever."

"Why won't you let us try to help?"

"Don't you get it, Wren?" Monroe snapped. "I've spent the past few decades trying to get rid of it. This... this thing inside of me. I can't live a normal life. I can't have friends or lovers that last more than a night because I'm terrified they'll learn what I am and leave, or worse, turn me in."

"Not to put too fine a point on it here, but we know, and we're still here, and we aren't turning you in," Jaime said plainly. "You can trust us."

"Please. Do you know how many doctors have said that to me? Who promised a cure, only to make one half-hearted attempt and take off with my parents' money? My parents, who gave up on trying to cure me when I was nineteen and moved to the south of France, leaving me alone with nothing more than money in the bank."

Wren reached for Monroe's hand again, but this time, she pulled away. "No. You can't help me, neither of you can. I've spoken to every expert who could help me. I've scoured libraries and medical data, looking for some... for some scrap of evidence that I could be rid of this and just be *normal*."

"What if this *is* normal... for you?" Jaime offered.

Monroe glared at them, her lip trembling with emotion. She snatched the box of donuts from the counter and marched past both of them, up the stairs, and slamming the bedroom door.

"Well done, genius," Wren spat. "I told you not to say anything, and you blurted it out the first chance you got."

"I'm trying to help!"

"She's obviously scared, wouldn't you be? Two strangers announcing your biggest secret wouldn't make you feel a little off-balance?"

Jaime scoffed. "I find that having everything out in the open is healthier for everyone involved."

"You didn't have to suggest that she'd kill me."

"It was hyperbole!"

"She was so gentle that night, and petrified, she never would have hurt me, I could feel it. It's why I helped her in the first place."

"Weren't you scared?"

"Of course I was scared," Wren hissed. "But I was scared of you at first, too, and now look, we're practically joined at the hip and I couldn't get rid of you if I tried."

"Why were you scared of me?"

"You're loud, Jaime. You're loud and you're confident and for wallflowers like me, that's intimidating."

"You've never been a wallflower."

"Tell that to the graduating class of 2008." Wren sighed, rubbing at her dry, sleep-deprived eyes. "I don't want her to go."

"You *do* like her, don't you?"

A flush crept up Wren's neck. "I don't know. Maybe."

"Tell that to your face," Jaime replied with a smirk. "Alright, listen, where's this meeting?"

"City Hall. Six tonight."

"I have a plan, but you have to trust me."

"That sounds ominous."

"Trust me, Wren. I know what I'm doing. I've seen enough rom-coms to craft the perfect setting to profess your love."

"Stop it. I just want to convince her not to leave. Not yet, anyway."

"Sure. That too."

Jaime shoved a donut in their mouth and grabbed keys from the counter. "I have to go to work now, but I'll see you later. I'll pick you up at Joe's after your shift. Are you getting the bus?"

Wren nodded. "Yeah, in thirty minutes. I still have to shower, I look like a gremlin."

"But a cute gremlin. Don't eat all the glazed, save some for the Bear upstairs."

Chapter 10

"We now call this meeting to order. Council, is everyone accounted for?" the bored secretary asked.

"All present," a woman with a severe blond bob replied in a chirpy voice. "A warm welcome to our visitor, Ms. Monroe Chase of Syndicorp. Thank you for joining us this evening."

"Let's get this over with," a man in a plaid jacket grumbled. "We all know we don't want that company here in Roanoak Falls."

Monroe bit back a beleaguered sigh and plastered on a smile. "If I can have just a few moments of your time, I think you will see why we are so interested in your town." She passed out pamphlets to all seven members of the council, saving one for herself as a reference. "As you may well know, Syndicorp is one of the leading employers and job creators in the country. Known for our practice of internal promotion, we value our workforce."

"Get to the point," the grouchy man said. "I don't want to be here all night, and neither do the rest of them. They're all just too polite to say it."

"Right. Well, if you turn to page four, I've laid out our proposal for the area. Two locations, one here in town, taking over the empty library building and surrounding lots, and the other five miles away on the highway."

"How much green space would the highway location require?" one of them asked.

"The minimal amount. We pride ourselves on our commitment to environmental conservation." The words, the lies, were ash in her mouth. She snapped the band against her wrist and carried on. "It would be profitable to the town to take in corporation taxes for the first three years, to depreciate the next eighteen months along with the building's value."

"How many jobs?" another one chimed in.

"At least five hundred."

The council members murmured amongst themselves.

"Bullshit," the angry man said. "I've seen what your kind does to small towns like this one. You gut them. You scrape everything that's good out and leave ugly, empty buildings." He tossed the pamphlet onto the long table with a thwap. "I say no."

"But Ben—" the blond woman protested. "Unemployment in the town has been a problem ever since the lumber mill closed. I don't think we can afford to pass up an opportunity like this."

"Come on, Margaret, you know that we don't even have the authority to sign off on something like this, we'd need the mayor's signature, and you know as well as I do that we are currently fresh out of mayors."

"Actually, your town's codices imply that in the event there is no serving mayor, the council can choose to act in the interest of the residents," Monroe interrupted, the words rehearsed and empty. The beast inside of her began to stir.

"My answer is still an emphatic no, and it's going to keep being a no. You're wasting your time here, Ms. Chase."

"We choose towns based on strict criteria of eligibility and viability for the store locations. Roanoak Falls could be an up-and-coming area in just eighteen months, with lower unemployment rates than neighboring areas and higher property values."

"Do you actually believe the bull crap that comes out of your mouth?"

"Ben!" an older woman at the end of the table said with a gasp. "Language!"

"Apologies, ma'am," he said, tipping his faded, torn baseball cap. "I get worked up about keeping this place out of their clutches. I just wish I could get you all to agree with me. We all want what's best for the town or we wouldn't be here, I realize that, but my mind is made up."

"On page eleven are our projections for growth around these new stores. With these superstores come opportunities for small, service-based busi-nesses like salons, mechanics, or restaurants," Monroe continued, snapping the band at her wrist three more times. She was getting too frustrated. "I would think that even a staunchly opposed citizen would be in support of entrepreneurship." It was all a script, rehearsed, the lines delivered in dozens of small towns all across the country, one after another, securing the deal and moving on to the next one.

"I feel that Ben may have a point," the older lady said, tapping the pink eraser of her pencil against the laminate desktop. "I may not always agree with how he delivers his points, but I cannot fault his dedication to this council. I'm sorry, Ms. Chase, but my answer is also no."

Monroe blinked, already imagining the irate phone call she'd get from Steve in twenty minutes. She'd get demoted, or worse, fired, and without work, what did she even have? Nothing. "Is there anything we could add to the table to change your minds?"

"Hell no," Ben said, shoving the papers away from him. "Not even if you offered us all under the table bribes."

"That's not something we do at Syndicorp."

He glared. "You and I both know that's not true."

"Hmm." Monroe was caught in a lie, not that he knew it for sure. It hadn't been out of the question to incentivize council members, mayors, or city planners to agree with Syndicorp's plan, but she'd never done it herself. "What are your main concerns, if I may ask?

"The destruction of this town. All the small businesses that have been here for generations, gone. Wiped out, replaced with generic labels in a cheaply built box of a store, sold by underpaid workers." He clenched his hand into a fist. "We need infrastructure and investment, not whatever devil's contract you're peddling." He frowned. "Nothing personal."

"I can provide a case study—"

The door to city hall swung wide, revealing Amber Pennington, her designer bag nestled in the crook of her elbow. "Good evening, Council."

"Can we help you?" the secretary asked. "We're in a session."

"Of course. Why do you think I'm here? As the next mayor, it's my duty to keep apprised of the town's goings-on, wouldn't you agree?"

"We haven't even had the election yet," Ben said dismissively. "This isn't an open session."

"I don't think you want to start off on the wrong foot here. I am running unopposed."

"For now."

Amber sniffed. "What do you mean, for now?"

"I mean, the deadline for signatures isn't until Monday."

"I've been PTA president for almost a decade. Every parent will vote for me. We all know that I'm going to be the next mayor, and I think it's of the town's best interest that I be included in these meetings going forward."

The old lady stood. "If we bend the rules for you, then we'd have to bend them for everyone, and that sets a dangerous precedent. I'm sure you'd agree."

"I've already been in talks with someone from Syndicorp to bring Roanoak Falls into the twenty-first century. I'm sure you're all aware that the mayor's decision can overrule that of the council."

"Who?" Monroe asked. "Because I'm from Syndicorp, and I've never spoken to you on the subject."

"You're with Syndicorp?" Wren was standing in the doorway, her face a painting of betrayal. She threw down a bouquet of flowers onto the floor and clenched her fists. "Why didn't you tell me?"

"I'm sorry, who the hell are you?" Amber demanded. "I was assured by Marcie that I was the top priority in securing the tenancies."

Marcie. Of course he sent Marcie anyway, Steve, the complete snake. "Wren, just let me explain—"

"Explain what? You basically lied to my face."

Amber stepped between them. "How do you two even know each other?"

"I bought a shop-vac," Monroe replied, her tone gritty with strain. She had to get the hell out of there, or things were going to go bad, and fast. "Thank you all for your time this evening. Clearly I have to—Wren, wait!"

"Forget it."

"I have to liaise with my colleague," Monroe said, gathering her things and heading for the door. "Mrs. Pennington, always a pleasure."

"Hang on. Where do you think you're going? Are you even going to explain the pamphlet to me? I'm the future mayor, I'll have you know—"

"Uh huh, Marcie can fill you in." Though the sky had a tinge of orange at the horizon when she'd entered the building, it was thick and velvety blue now, pierced only by the bright, cold beams of the moon. It felt like a white-hot flame against her skin. "Wren?" she called out. "Wren, let me explain!"

"Go away," Wren replied, flinging open the door of Jaime's car. "I thought—it doesn't matter what I thought. Aren't you leaving, anyway?"

"I—it's complicated, but I was going to leave, you're the one who—" Monroe gasped from the pain. No. Not again. Not so soon after the last time, she'd be laid up for weeks.

Concern flickered over Wren's face before her eyes hardened. "I hope you do get caught. Maybe then this town won't end up like a trash heap, discarded by your crappy company." She got into the car and slammed the door, the engine roaring into life.

Monroe staggered to her car, taking off her heeled boots. The wet sludge of the parking lot seeped into her tights and squished between her toes, frosty and disgusting. There was a small section of woods, but she'd have to make a run for it. Grabbing her duffel bag, she sprinted across the parking lot, heaving herself over the low wooden fence at the edge of the manicured lawn.

Trees loomed in the distance, welcoming her into their grasping, reaching limbs, bare with the frost, laden with heavy snow. She was almost ankle deep in it, but the heat of the coming shift kept her from feeling her fragile skin crack from the cold. The thicket was dense and deep, so much so that less than twenty paces in, she'd already lost her way.

The undergrowth here hadn't been trimmed back in at least twenty years, maybe longer. Brittle thorns tore are her clothing, and her shifting ligaments tore at her nerve endings. She let herself moan through the pain, soft and muffled as she bit the sleeve of her thick wool coat.

She stripped, saving her clothes this time, tears leaking from her eyes as fur blossomed from beneath her skin and her form twisted, mangled until she was a beast again. The nearly full moon hung high in the sky, piercing, menacing. All she knew was fear, despite the cover of the trees. There might be hunters in these woods.

She lay in the snow, her snout buried in the earth, waiting for it to be over. Hunger chewed through her, leaving her ravenous and struggling. There was no easy food in here, and she didn't have the energy to hunt. She hadn't shifted this close together in years. She thought she had a handle on it. She was wrong. When a branch snapped behind her, she knew that it wouldn't be good.

Chapter 11

Wren sat at an empty residential intersection, waiting for... well, what was she waiting for, exactly? Guilt nagged at her. She shouldn't have left Monroe in the parking lot, not like that. Even if she *was* a liar. A liar whose job it was to jeopardize the entire town.

"Damn it anyway," she grunted, pulling a u-turn in the middle of the road. Her phone rang, and she pulled to the side to answer it. "What?" she snapped.

"No need for that tone with me, Wren, I just needed to know if you were coming back with my car anytime soon."

"Things didn't go as planned."

"Did she leave?"

"She works for Syndicorp."

Jaime let out a long hiss. "Yikes. Come pick me up, we'll go raid the grocery store for ice cream and booze."

"She didn't leave. She's in that small patch of trees behind town hall."

"What the hell is she doing there?"

"Shifting."

"Shift—and you *left* her there? Don't you know what kinds of people we have living around here? They have *guns*, Wren!"

"I know, I know! I'm already heading back."

"Wait—swing by and pick me up, you can't be far."

"Why?"

"Maybe I can help keep a lookout, at least."

Wren pulled another about-face. "I'll be there in three minutes. Be outside. Bring whatever food is in the house and ready to eat, she'll need it." She tossed the phone into the cup holder and drove ten miles over the speed limit, which was fifteen miles an hour faster than she would usually drive.

The streetlights illuminated Jaime already waiting at the end of the driveway, their arms filled with paper grocery bags and totes hanging off their elbows. "Took you long enough," they said, throwing the food in back and climbing into the passenger seat. "Let's go."

"Maybe you should drive, I—"

"Wren! Just go!"

She stamped on the gas, the tires protesting against the icy streets, slick from the day's melted snow. "I never should have left her there."

"That's for damn sure. I thought you *liked* her!"

"I do—I did! But she works for *them*, and they're trying to gut the whole of Roanoak Falls, and—"

"And what? You and I both know it's inevitable."

"That's a hell of a depressing thing to think."

Jaime brushed a stray lock of hair from their cheek. "I'm a realist, you know that. We both know they've been sniffing around here for years. It's no surprise they're trying to swoop in just after Mayor Kersche left. They were never able to even get a meeting before."

"That doesn't excuse it."

"Wren, you know that I love you as though you were my own blood sister, but I think Monroe might have bigger problems right now than her job."

"I know that, obviously, but—"

"Take the next left, it's a shortcut."

"It says residents only."

"Wren!"

She jerked the car to the left. "Fine, alright! Pardon me for following the rules!"

"It's barely even a real rule!" Jaime shot back. "Relax, we're almost there. Park at the end, out of view of the police station's CCTV."

"And how do you know where that is?"

"I've lived a colorful life."

Wren threw the car into park, fumbling to yank the keys from the ignition.

"Just go, I'll catch up. Go!"

She took off running, vaulting over a half-rotted fence, and disappearing into the trees. It was almost pitch-black, the moon's beams barely penetrating through the empty branches. "Monroe?" she called out. "It's us! Don't be scared!"

The toe of her boot caught on a root, sending her sprawling. She squinted into the darkness, willing her eyes to adjust. She reached for her phone, using the dim display to light the surrounding darkness. Turning on the flash, she looked around for any sign of Monroe.

The rustle of the dense underbrush set her teeth on edge, her jaw clamped shut. "Is anyone there? Monroe? Jaime?" There was no answer, except for the deep, guttural growl that emanated from beyond her sight. "Monroe?" she said again, her voice wavering. "I really hope that's you, because if it's not—"

She shined the light around, but saw nothing. The deep expanse of the small woods was impenetrable by a phone light. Bracing her hand against the ground, her skin slid across the snow, coated with something sticky and warm. Wren nearly retched at the sight of the thick blood on her hand, and soaking through the knees of her patterned tights.

"Monroe, please," she whispered into the dark.

"Wren!" Jaime called from the tree line. "Where are you?"

"Don't come any closer. I think she's in here, but she's not... herself."

"Come out! Back up the way you came! Follow my voice!"

"Shut up!" Wren shouted back, her voice caught in her throat. "I don't want to scare her."

"I don't want her to eat you!" Jaime threw three bags of potato wedges into the woods. "See if she wants these!"

She reached for one of the bags, crawling along the ground, the light on her phone pointed at the wet, snowy moss on the thicket's floor. The bear huffed out of sight, and the sound of a cracking bone sent shivers down Wren's spine.

"What was that?" Jaime hissed, their voice echoing across the empty parking lot.

"I don't know." Wren dug her fingers through the dirt, looking for the food.

"I don't think I want to know."

"Shit. Cops."

"Get rid of them!"

"They don't like me."

"They're going to like a bear even less. Make something up, Jaime!"

"Fine!" they whispered angrily. "Good evening, officers. What can I do for you?"

"We've had reports of vandalism in this area. Someone keeps spray painting the side of one of the empty buildings along Main Street."

"It's not me, I don't even have paint on me."

"What's in your pockets?"

"Potatoes."

One of the officers shined a light into the woods. "Say what now?"

"Potatoes. I like carbs. I'm a cross-country runner. Carb loading, you know."

"My wife does marathons. You do any marathons?"

"No, I prefer not to run competitively."

Wren barely even breathed in those moments, willing the police to leave them all alone. If they found Monroe, animal control would be there in twenty minutes.

Jaime sauntered across the snow, their knee-high boots caked to the ankle in sludge. "Vandalism, you say? I might have seen something the other night, you know."

"You did?"

"Oh, yeah, couple of shady looking... teenagers. I could come across to the station and make a statement, if that's helpful?"

"Yeah. Yeah, good idea. We always knew you'd wise up, eventually."

Even through the thick brush, Wren saw Jaime's jaw tighten. She'd owe them for this, and big. Assuming she wasn't about to be torn limb from limb befriending a Bear, that was.

When the three were out of sight, she dug around again for the food. Jaime had taken the rest with them. The Bear snuffled around, lapping up what Wren could only assume was blood. Her stomach turned at the thought. What—or who—had Monroe killed?

Her fingers closed around the bag of potato wedges, the condensation inside the plastic sparkling in the sparse moon beams. "It's just me, you're okay," she sang lightly, as though she were talking to a puppy. "I have some food for you." Her heart pounded in her ears with every step she took towards the sounds further in the trees.

"Don't be upset. I got rid of the others. It's just you and me, now." She reached into the bag and fished out a potato, cold now, but still smelling of garlic powder and paprika.

Taking another step forward, her boot squelched into something uncomfortably springy, and unlike snow or moss. She twisted her wrist towards the ground, shining the dim light at what was under her feet.

She gasped, stumbling backwards, dropping the bag of wedges. It was a deer, an old one by the looks of it, freshly killed. At least it wasn't a person. "Monroe, it's okay."

The Bear stepped out from a hedge, its back eyes shining in the reflection of the phone's flash. It snuffled around the bag, using a huge paw to hold the plastic to the ground and rip it open, sending potato wedges skipping across the ground. It ate them quietly, the quiet huffs sending bursts of steam into the air.

Wren slid closer along the wet moss and held out her hand. "It's me."

It was almost deafening when the Bear roared, scattering a flock of crows in a nearby tree. Wren bit back a scream, sure she was about to die. What was the advice to survive a bear attack? Did it even matter when a bear was on its hind legs, towering over you, ready to strike?

She whimpered. "Please, I'm sorry. I never should have left you on your own like that."

The Bear returned its front paws to the earth and padded closer, staring at her with curiosity, as though it had never seen her before.

Wren leaned forward, resting a hand on the bear's snout. "It's me." When the Bear didn't react, she reached up to pet its ears, gently, running her fingertips over the coarse fur. "I'm not going to hurt you."

The Bear's eyes flickered with recognition and wrenched away, tripping over its own paws, grunting and snorting in distress. It disappeared into the brush again, and after a few moments, Monroe's voice lilted across the softly falling snow, strained with effort. "Please go."

"I'm sorry, I—"

"It's dangerous for you. I'm... not myself." She groaned with pain. "Wren, I need you to go."

"I'm not leaving you like this."

"You have to. I might hurt you, and I... I could never live with myself if something happened."

"You wouldn't hurt me, I saw it in your eyes, please—"

"I would! I would. I almost did."

"But—"

"Leave!" Monroe roared, her voice gravelly and tight with emotion. "Leave now!"

* * *

Wren stood at the edge of the small wood, shivering in the bitter cold.

"What happened?" Jaime asked, approaching from the parking lot.

"Where are the cops?"

"I got rid of them. They're just bored and looking to entertain themselves by rounding up some delinquent youths."

"Thank you."

"Where is she?"

"Still in the woods. She told me to leave."

Jaime leaned against a large boulder, hiding their face inside a long, fluffy scarf. "Is she a..."

"Yeah. I... think she killed something."

"It's not a person, is it? If it is, I hope it's my asshole boss."

"It's a deer."

"Well, that's not really that big of a deal, is it? It's not like you're a vegetarian."

"No, it's just…" Wren chewed on her lip, cracked from the freezing temperatures. "I don't know. I don't want to leave her in there alone, but she made it clear she didn't want me there."

"Should we stand guard? I got rid of the police, but you never know if a pair of hormonal teenagers are looking for somewhere to—"

"Ew."

"It's reality, Wren, and teenagers have big mouths. One of them posts it to their feed, before you know it the whole damn town is here."

"You'd think it was too cold for that."

"It's never too cold for that when you're determined enough. Alright, well, I'll get the camping chairs from the trunk of the car. What should we do with the food?"

"I think she's probably had her fill, now."

"Excellent, more for me." Jaime walked to the car, humming, their voice carrying gently across the snow-filled air. They returned with the chairs, food, and a thermos of tea.

"You brought a thermos?"

"I like to be prepared. I grew up in scouts."

"How did you even have time to prepare that?"

Jaime popped the chairs' legs into position and sat them on the snow. "Was already making tea when you called. Here, have a sip, you look half-frozen."

"I feel it."

"We should go by our place tomorrow, make sure the pipes haven't burst."

Wren groaned. "Why even tempt fate by saying that out loud?"

"Better than tempting it by ignoring the problem entirely, wouldn't you agree?"

"I guess." She took a sip of the tea, allowing its warmth to slide down her throat and into her core. "I didn't like how she looked at me, Jaime."

"What do you mean?"

"Angry, maybe. Almost feral." She sighed. "Not like last time."

"Maybe she just needs some time."

"I don't know how I didn't realize that she works for Syndicorp. It was staring me in the face the entire time, and I missed it."

Jaime shrugged. "It doesn't matter, Wren. What's done is done."

"It's not a done deal yet. Roanoak Falls might still have a chance."

"If she's the one heading it up, maybe it wouldn't be so bad. She has a good heart."

"I know she does, but she's not going to be the head honcho, you know? Hell, she'll probably be out of here like a shot the second she has the chance." Wren kicked at a large piece of gravel, sending it skittering into a bush. "She wanted to go already."

"Only because I opened my big mouth."

Wren held the open thermos close to her face, absorbing the steam before it dissipated into the air. "I do wish you'd kept it to yourself a little while longer."

"I thought getting everything out in the open was healthier. I don't care if she turns into a bear every month, and clearly, neither do you, but she's carrying that weight around with her. I can't even imagine the weight of it." They sighed. "I'm sorry. I said I wouldn't say anything, but I did because I thought I knew better. Clearly, I didn't."

"Thank you," Wren replied. She crossed her legs, huddled into herself. "And it's not every month. She said it's been a year since the last time."

Jaime opened a bag of chips, crunching loudly as they chewed. "That's not how Weres work."

"Oh, because you've met so many of them, right? Do you have a secret pack of Wolves that you hang around with while I'm at work?"

"No, I just mean, it seems strange, that's all. From what you said, it seems triggered by a lunar cycle, right? So how come she doesn't shift the rest of the month?"

"I don't know, she holds it back."

"Seems unhealthy to live like that."

"Because eating raw deer in the woods is the pinnacle of health?" Wren asked, stealing the bag of chips.

"Some people would pay a lot of money for that experience. I bet some influencer has already marketed it as a detox that cleanses your pancreas, or something."

"You're very calm about all of this."

"What's one more weirdo? You and me, we've never fit in. You walk around looking like a fairy who lost her way half the time, in your cute little outfits and sweaters. People don't even know how to address me half the time. Who cares if Monroe is a Bear? She put a roof over our heads and fed us. That's more than our own damn parents did."

Wren twisted her ring. "Yeah."

"Pass the thermos, I'm freezing. It's going to be a long night."

Chapter 12

Monroe shivered as she pulled on her fleece-lined tracksuit, shoving her feet into the rubber boots. She'd tried to wipe most of the blood off her face with snow, but her camera phone showed that she hadn't been very successful.

Shame ate at her, gnawing at her insides. What if she had attacked Wren? She'd barely been able to pull the shift back for thirty seconds before it overtook her again. Her muscles throbbed, pulsating with the same punishing rhythm as her head. Sunlight glared off the fresh snow and pounded into her brain.

Her mouth was parched, thick with saliva and the taste of iron. She retched, bringing up part of the night's prey. Seeing it made her bring up more. It had been nearly a decade since she'd lost control like that, since she had allowed herself to fail, and allowed feral instincts to cloud reason.

With shaky hands, she packed the duffel and slung it over her shoulder, staggering out of the woods and praying that no one would see her. The world spun around her, and the dizziness threatened to make her vomit for a third time.

Voices carried on the wind, sending a rock plummeting into her stomach. How would she explain being covered in blood, leaving a forest? And the dead deer? They'd lock her up in a heartbeat, no questions asked. She turned in the other direction, stumbling, desperate to get to her car.

"Monroe? Monroe, wait!" Wren came dashing across the snow, blanket in hand. "You look frozen, here, have this."

"What are you doing here?"

"I—we—waited. For you. To make sure you were okay."

"I'm fine."

Wren raised a concerned eyebrow. "You don't look fine."

"I could have killed you both."

"You didn't."

"I told you to go!"

"And I did—but I wasn't about to let some stranger stumble into the woods."

Monroe jerked away from the blanket. "Why, afraid I'd tear them to shreds?"

"No." Wren blinked at her. "Afraid they would report you. Obviously."

"You saw what I did in there."

"Yes."

"I'm a monster, Wren. I'm out of control, I—I can't be trusted around people or… or anything. I should be locked up."

"I think we can all agree that's a gross overexaggeration, can't we?" Jaime said, folded up camping chairs tucked under their arm. "It's a deer, Love, not a toddler. If you hadn't gotten to it, the hunters would have. Or the semi trucks on the highway."

"It's monstrous."

"It's nature."

Monroe turned away, trying to rub the remnants of blood from her face with the sleeve of her hoodie. "It's disgusting."

"We can debate semantics later, but you are in no condition to drive. Come on, let's get you home, and we'll order enough food to fill a dozen Bears. How does that sound?"

"My car…"

Jaime tossed a set of keys to Wren. "Here, drive mine back. I know you don't like unfamiliar cars. I'll take Monroe's."

"It's a rental, the insurance—"

"Then you'll ride with me. Wren, maybe you should stop at the store and pick up some juice? She's going to need some serious hydration after the night she's had."

"I'm fine," Monroe insisted. "I'm fine to drive, and I'm fine in general." Her vision swam, and she had to steady herself on Jaime's shoulder.

"My ass. You get behind the wheel of a car and you're going to do more damage than you ever have as a Bear." Jaime gestured at the car door. "Your chariot awaits."

She didn't bother to argue anymore. They were right, she shouldn't be driving. Jaime opened the car door for her, and she slid into the passenger seat. "There are seat warmers if you switch them on, there on the left."

"Oh hell yes," Jaime said with glee in their voice. "My ass is frozen solid."

The car roared into life, and in just a few seconds, the leather radiated warmth into Monroe's flesh. She couldn't deny that the heat felt great on her skin. "De-icer fluid is on the right."

"Lord, is this how the other half lives? Butt warmers, de-icers, hell, I'm lucky if my car even starts when it gets this cold. I swear, I spend half the winter chipping frost from the windshield."

"It does make a difference in a place like this."

"I'll say." Jaime pulled the car onto the road, turning left while Wren turned right towards the store. "I'm sure she won't be long."

"Mm," was all she could reply. The motion of the car was making her stomach roil with bile and whatever else was in there. She grimaced.

"So. You're a Bear." Jaime turned onto Main Street, but it was quiet this early in the morning. "I have to admit, I'm a little jealous."

"You shouldn't be jealous that you aren't cursed."

"I just mean—"

"It's singularly the worst thing about me, fills every waking moment, and causes me a great deal of pain. It's ignorant to suggest that it's some kind of fun hobby."

They drove in silence for a few moments. "I'm sorry."

"Thank you."

"Sometimes, in my attempts to reassure people, it comes off like I am minimizing. Wren tells me to be more aware of it, so, I'm sorry."

"How long have you known each other?"

"I don't know, ten years now? Feels like I've known her for a lifetime. She's like a sister to me. I'd throw myself in front of a lion for her."

"Or a Bear?"

Jaime glanced sideways at her. "It doesn't seem like there's any need to protect her from a Bear."

"Last night suggests otherwise."

"We were right there the whole night, Monroe. If you'd wanted to have us as a snack, you would have."

"You don't know that."

"I do, actually, because I am driving this very nice car back to the house, and not resting gently in your tummy."

"Please don't talk about my stomach, I feel fragile enough as it is."

"Better or worse than a hangover?"

Monroe coughed out a laugh. "Like the worst hangover you've ever had, except it lasts for days." She checked her phone. "Twenty-seven missed calls from my boss."

"Sounds like you're the favorite."

"More like the black sheep after last night." She leaned back against the headrest. "How angry is she that I didn't tell her?"

"Oh, she's angry, all right. But I think she'll forgive you, if you play your cards right."

"And what does that look like?"

Jaime smirked, pulling into the driveway. "Ask her on a date."

Blood rushed into Monroe's face, and she turned towards the window to hide the flush in her cheeks. "I uh—I didn't—she wouldn't—"

"She would. Right, I expect you want to clean up. I'll go run you a bath and get those clothes into the laundry for you. I'll order some food—not much is delivering at this time of the morning other than breakfast, is that okay?"

"Pancakes."

"Pancakes it is—"

"And scrambled eggs. And French toast. Oh, and bacon. Please." She tossed them her wallet. "Use the black card."

* * *

"You alright in there?" Jaime called through the bathroom door.

Monroe opened one eye and groaned. "I fell asleep in the bath."

"We were worried you got lost on the way back to the kitchen. It can be a treacherous set of stairs, I've heard."

"Ha ha." She tugged on the plug, the now lukewarm water draining away. She sniffed the air. "What's cooking?"

"Wren's cooking. Nowhere was delivering, and I promise you, you don't want me anywhere near the kitchen. I manage to burn water."

"I know what you mean." Monroe wrapped herself in a large, fluffy towel, heated from the rack on the wall, and sighed at the delicious warmth. "I'll be right down."

"Your phone has been ringing off the hook. Is that a problem?"

She groaned. "Yes. But it's going to be more of a problem if I call him back before I've eaten. I'm liable to quit on the spot the second he answers. No doubt he's pissed that I didn't get the sign off last night."

"They've really got their sights set on Roanoak Falls, haven't they?"

"Yes. Quotas and all that."

"Mm. Alright, see you downstairs." Their footsteps faded down the steps, laughter between the two of them bouncing off the high ceilings in the open kitchen.

Monroe stepped into fresh clothes, tight black jeans, thick hiking socks, a white long sleeved tee, and a green crushed velvet blazer that she'd planned on wearing on the flight back. She'd have to do laundry, now that the deal was going to take even longer.

Damned Steve, and damned Marcie, always interfering. Now she had to deal with a pissed off city council and a power-hungry mayor-to-be who had probably already made verbal agreements with Marcie. Monroe sighed heavily, pulling her blow-dried hair back into its familiar neat bun at the nape of her neck. Complicated business proposals were the last thing she needed at the moment.

She grimaced, running her hand over her ribs beneath her shirt before she tucked it in. The strange patch of fur had receded, but was still there, ever present. Looming over her like a dark cloud, threatening her with another unplanned shift.

Pulling the bedroom door open to the hallway, her senses were filled with an explosion of smells, sweet and savory all at once. Her stomach growled angrily, greedy for food.

"What's cooking?" she asked, leaning against the door frame. "Smells divine."

"We couldn't manage takeout, so I went a little wild," Wren replied. She had a smudge of flour on her cheek, and Monroe reached out to brush it off.

"Thank you."

"You don't even know what I made, yet!"

"I can already tell it's going to be amazing."

Wren blushed, biting her lip. "Jaime said you asked for pancakes, so there's that, but I made a fresh berry compote for the top because the store was out of maple syrup. There are eggs, too, and bacon, but I also made cheddar scones—there's a lightly herbed compound butter for those—and I also whipped up some spiced crumble coffee cake for later."

"You've made so much—"

"I forgot, there's also cinnamon rolls proofing in the oven, and a small batch of pear and cardamom muffins that just finished cooling."

"How the hell did you do all that already?"

Wren shrugged. "This kitchen has a good mixer."

"She's being modest," Jaime interrupted. "She managed it because she's amazingly talented."

"You should run a bakery," Monroe said, an eyebrow raised in appreciation.

"I wish," Wren replied, a sadness settling at the corners of her eyes. "But anyway, let's eat before the pancakes get cold."

Monroe filled her plate, heaping with glorious, delicious carbohydrates, just what she needed after a difficult shift. Her bones ached to her core, but the hot, sweet food dulled the pain, or at least, made her forget for a few moments. "This is so delicious. How did you know that raspberries are my favorite?"

"I read that bears like them," Wren answered.

"You... chose them for that reason?"

"Sure."

"I'm not really a bear, you know. I'm a human. Humans can like raspberries, too."

Wren's brow furrowed. "Of course." She chewed thoughtfully for a moment. "Are you upset?"

"Not upset. It's a gorgeous meal, the best breakfast I've ever eaten."

"You don't have to say that."

"I'm not," Monroe said, wiping her mouth with a napkin before getting up to fill her plate again. "I am being completely honest. I've never had pancakes so fluffy, nor scones so light and airy. Usually they're—"

"Too dense and crumbly," Wren finished. "I agree. I'm not opposed to density, but not at the cost of texture and flavor."

"It's a nice pairing with the sweetness of the other dishes, that savory saltiness." Monroe bit into her second muffin. "And these are divine."

"I'm glad you like them."

Monroe held Wren's gaze for just a moment longer than she should have, but the way the light was cascading across her face gave her a radiant glow that was hard to look away from.

"Well, I'm off to work," Jaime announced abruptly, brushing crumbs from their shirt.

"You didn't tell me you had work," Wren protested.

"I forgot. It's last minute. Picked up a shift. Excellent breakfast, ten stars, I'm taking these muffins for lunch, don't try to stop me."

"On another day, I might fight you for them," Monroe said. "But today there are scones, and the scones have my heart."

The front door clicked shut, and they both stared at their plates for a moment. "I guess you have work to do," Wren announced, starting to clear the dishes. "I won't disturb you."

"I'm sorry. I should have told you, I just... I didn't want you to think badly of me. It was clear from our first meeting how you feel about Syndicorp."

"I shouldn't have overreacted."

"You have nothing to apologize for." Monroe sighed, sitting back in her chair. "Leave the dishes for me, I'll wash them up."

"No, that's okay—"

"I insist. You made everything, it's only fair."

"Are you sure you're feeling up to it?"

"It's a distraction from having to call my boss, at least. I'd wash a dozen kitchens' worth of dirty dishes if it meant I didn't have to call him back." She stood, taking the stack from Wren and setting them in the sink, the hot water already running. "You know, my entire adult life, work has been the only thing to give me any sort of purpose or meaning. It's going to be... strange." She dunked a dish into the hot soapy water, feeling words form on her tongue. "If you aren't busy later.." she trailed off, her heart suddenly in her throat. Why was her pulse racing? Was another shift coming? "On second thought—"

"Do you want to go to the festival with me later?" Wren asked, spinning the ring around her finger. "Maybe this time we can see the lights."

"I'd love to, it's just..."

"You're afraid you'll shift again."

Monroe cleared her throat. "Yes."

"I'll pack snacks this time, and your job is to not think about work, alright?"

"Okay." Monroe tried to play it cool, but found herself grinning. "I'll pick you up from work at seven."

Chapter 13

"Wren, have you seen where those extra Christmas lights went?"

"They're in the storeroom, on the left, third shelf in the back," she replied.

Mr. Ranelli harrumphed quietly. "Who put them *there*?"

"You did, sir."

"Clearly I was not of sound mind when I did that. I'm going to put the lights up outside, maybe it will cheer us up."

"Are you feeling down today?"

"Oh, you know," he said. "Just not sure what things are going to look like, come the new year. I heard that Mrs. Pennington is steaming ahead with that Syndicorp woman."

Wren flinched. "Yeah, I heard that, too."

"I reckon nothing can stop her now. Once she gets an idea in her head, the rest of us have to go along with it. Remember when she wanted to ban cupcakes at the school? It was all over the local paper and everything."

"I remember." Wren set a box on the shelf, straightening it. "Cut out any possibility of me offering custom orders."

"Do you ever think of getting out of here? Pack up, move somewhere else, forget all this?"

"I did that once. I ended up here in Roanoak Falls."

The bells on the door jingled with a saccharine cheer, and an icy gust blew in around her legs.

"Wren Jackson, you didn't come to my campaign launch," Amber pouted, a hand on her hip. "You promised!"

"I said that I would try," Wren protested. "Something came up."

"What came up?"

"Just... something."

"It wasn't that Monroe woman I saw you arguing with, was it? I have it on good authority that she doesn't have this town's best interests at heart."

"Whose authority is that?"

"My contact at Syndicorp. She said that this deal should have been signed, sealed, and delivered last week. Yet here we are, with no agreement in hand, even now."

"Isn't that because the mayor resigned?"

"Please, Wren, don't be so silly. If she really wanted, she would have made the deal with me the day she arrived. It's not as though anyone is running against me. I'm a sure thing." Amber leaned against the cash counter, her dark, pin-straight hair brushing against the pale blue coat she was wearing. "This town is dying, we all know that."

Mr. Ranelli huffed quietly, disappearing into the back room. "Some of us aren't quite ready to give up yet," he grumbled.

Amber rolled her eyes. "What we really need here is investment. This Syndicorp deal is a gift, all wrapped up for Christmas. Jobs are what people need, and that's what they're offering. All we have to do is open the present."

"I don't know if everyone agrees with you."

"What about you, Wren? You agree with me, right?"

Wren turned away, twisting the ring on her thumb. "I wish we could pull together as a community, do more to entice tourists, maybe. I'm not sure we have to take the first *gift* that's offered. Trojan horses, and all that."

"This is how the world works, Darling, and two new super stores is the best offer Roanoak Falls is going to get. If we don't take it, I can guarantee this place will be a ghost town within five years. I don't want that, do you?"

"Of course not."

"Here," Amber said, laying a hand on Wren's shoulder and turning her around. "I had some pamphlets printed about my candidacy. Even though no one else is running, I wanted to do it right."

"Er—thanks, I guess."

"Maybe you could hand them out to the other local businesses for me? I'm sure they'll all want to know what their new mayor will do for them."

"Or you could... visit them yourself?" Wren suggested lightly, swallowing back irritation. "I'm sure they'd love to hear from you directly."

Amber pressed the pamphlets into her hand. "Thank you for offering to hand these out, I so appreciate it. It's nice to know that there's someone in this town I can count on. You know, we never set a day for our second date! People love seeing their candidates in stable, thriving relationships, you know."

"I'm just... really busy at work."

"Certainly doesn't *look* busy in here."

"Inventory."

"Hmm. Indeed. Well, I'll call you later, after closing, say? I can pick you up around eight again tonight."

Wren smiled, but there was no affection for Mrs. Pennington behind it. "I'm really sorry, but I have plans."

"Plans? What plans?"

"Dinner with... my friend. Jaime."

"You could reschedule. You already live in the same house, what more do you need?"

"Perhaps another time?"

"Tomorrow, then."

"I have to work," Wren lied, hoping that Mr. Ranelli wouldn't appear to call her out on her lie. "And I work closing the rest of the week."

"Lunch, then."

The door's bells jangled again, chaotic and unpredictable. "Wren, I'm here to have lunch with you," Jaime announced.

"Lunch? I thought you were having dinner," Amber challenged.

Jaime raised an eyebrow. "We are," they lied, immediately catching on. "Is it a crime to share two meals in a day? It's nearly Christmas, after all, it's not a crime against the state to spend time with my best friend, is it?"

"Sure." Amber laid another stack of pamphlets on the counter. "Thank you for offering to hand these out, Wren. I appreciate it. I'll pop by tomorrow to see when you're free for that date." She left, the door almost slamming from the force.

"What was *that* all about?" Jaime asked, scrunching up their nose. "And why did you agree to hand out pamphlets?"

Wren rolled her eyes. "I didn't. She's just very insistent."

"I have something important to tell you."

"Yeah, it must be for you to give up your lunch break to come all the way over here. What's going on? Is it—" she mouthed *Monroe* and lifted her eyebrows in question.

"Don't be ridiculous, of course it's nothing like that. You think I wouldn't just text you if it was an emergency? No, I knew I had to tell you this in person, so it would be harder for you to say no."

"Spit it out."

"Okay, don't be mad."

"You aren't filling me with confidence here, Jaime."

"It's good! It's a good thing! You just have to promise you won't immediately say no."

Wren huffed. "Fine."

"So I was at work, and this cute couple came in. They're obviously not from around here, but whatever. They order food, I start to walk away, but for some reason I found myself listening to their conversation."

"I sincerely hope you aren't about to ask me to do something illegal."

"I would at the very least buy you a coffee before making you an accomplice, don't worry. No, they're getting married in the area next month!"

"Okay?"

"Married!"

"Are you going to explain?" Wren asked with a snort. "Or do I have to guess?"

"One of them was saying that they want a cake, but there's nowhere around here, and—"

"No."

Jaime made a pleading face, their knees bent, their hands held out as if in prayer. "Come on, Wren, this could be the break you've been waiting for!"

"One wedding? No. You know my policy, no wedding cakes. Too much risk."

"They seem really nice."

"So do most people, when the reality of planning a wedding hasn't quite set in yet."

"I sort of maybe almost kinda said that I knew someone who could help them."

"Jaime!" Wren protested. "Tell them no!"

"I also perhaps said they could meet you at the festival tonight."

"I'm going with Monroe tonight."

"Oh? With her, or *with* with her?"

"I... don't actually know."

"Did she ask you?"

"No, I asked her."

Jaime smirked. "I knew you liked her."

"Shut up. I'm already regretting it because there's no way we'd ever work. She works for them, and besides, she'll be out of this place the second she can."

"At least you're not stuck going on another weird date with Amber."

"No, I'm stuck juggling a not-date and, apparently, potential clients." Wren grimaced. "Thanks to you."

"I was trying to be helpful!"

"Too much, Jaime," she said. "What if they actually want me to make it?"

"Then that's good!"

"What if they hate it?"

Jaime flipped their scarf over their shoulder. "It's impossible, because your work is stunning. Second, even if they did hate it, then we just know that they are monsters with no taste."

"Can you cancel?"

"They're *really* nice. They tipped me forty percent."

"Damn."

"Just meet them, alright? If they have weird vibes, I'll get rid of them and never mention it again as long as I live. Also, I will owe you a favor."

"You already owe me several."

"Good, you can bank them."

Wren sighed. "Fine. Monroe is picking me up here at seven after I close. Where did you tell these people to meet us?"

"In town, near the clock tower. Honestly, Wren, I think they just wanted to meet some locals. They're from up north, they said, down to do a meet-the-parents type deal for the photographer."

"Alright, fine."

"I'm sorry for crashing your date."

"It's not a date."

Jaime tipped their hat. "It's definitely a date."

* * *

Wren's breath fogged the front window of the store as she locked up for the night.

"All ready?" Monroe asked, leaning against her car.

"As ready as I'll ever be. Jaime asked me to meet some people looking for a wedding cake or something in town. Is that okay?"

Monroe's face fell. "Oh, uh... yeah, of course. Sure. Just tell me where to park."

"Same place as last time is fine."

"A wedding cake, that's exciting?"

"I don't know about exciting." Wren slid into the passenger seat and buckled the seatbelt. "We'll see."

"Not a fan of commissions?"

"Weddings are important for a lot of people, and the cake is a centerpiece. Easy to mess up."

"You don't strike me as someone who'd mess that up. Trust me, I spent most of today wandering back and forth from the couch to the kitchen to eat more of those treats you left. I think I'm ruined for store-bought cinnamon rolls."

"The secret is in the double proof. Single just isn't good enough, the dough ends up tough."

"See? You know your stuff. I bet you'd make a gorgeous cake, one people would be proud of having in their photos." Monroe paused for a moment, lost in thought. "I really do think you should have your own bakery, you know. Have more faith in yourself, you clearly have the abilities."

"It's not as easy as all that, though, is it? I don't know the first thing about running a business, not to mention all the startup funds I'd need that I probably won't ever be able to save up."

"It will happen for you one day. I can just feel it."

Wren leaned her head against the window, watching the homes lit with festive lights fly past as they drove down the street. "You have a lot of confidence in someone you barely know."

"That's a hell of a thing to say, considering you had a lot of confidence I wouldn't rip off your arms for a snack."

"What happened last night?"

Monroe grimaced, keeping her eyes fixed on the road in front of them. "It's getting worse, I think."

"Worse how?"

"I used to have more control. Lately, things are setting me off. I don't know if it's work, or... this place..."

"Why would a location make it worse?"

"I don't know." Monroe sighed and flipped the radio off. "I don't really know anything about myself or my condition. No one has ever been able to give me the answers I want."

"That sounds really lonely."

"It is." The car's engine purred under the hood, even as they stopped at a traffic light. "These past few days with you and Jaime have been the most face-to-face interaction I've had in years."

"No girlfriends?" Wren asked, too interested in the answer.

"None that have lasted longer than a few weeks. They all left me in the end. Said I was too distant, not emotionally present enough."

"I wouldn't say that about you."

"There's nothing left to hide from you though, is there? You know the deep, dark secret."

"You never told any of them?"

Monroe shook her head, her eyes still on the road. "Not a single one. I couldn't risk it."

"Would you have told me if I hadn't seen it for myself?"

"No."

"Oh," Wren replied, trying not to feel hurt. "I understand."

"We're here. Are you ready?"

"As ready as I'll ever be for a consultation I never asked for and didn't want." Wren pulled her coat tighter around herself as a defense against the biting cold. "I'm sure this won't take too long."

"Wren!" Jaime called from the sidewalk, waving their arms wide. "Over here!" They looked so proud of themselves, so eager to help. Wren just hoped they weren't about to help her right into a huge disaster.

"Hi," one of the women said, smiling widely. "I'm Cat, and this is my wife-to-be, Andie."

"Nice to meet you both," Wren said. "You know Jaime, and this is my friend, Monroe."

Cat's eyes flickered with recognition, her brow furrowed. "Nice to meet you, too." She smiled again, tugging at the hem of her worn, faded hoodie. "We're from up north a ways, but we'll be getting married here in the spring. Andie's folks live about a twenty minute drive from here. Her mom can't take much time off on account of her job, so we decided to get married here."

"Congratulations!" Wren said. "I'm afraid my friend may have oversold my—"

"I'm sorry," Jaime interrupted, "but please ignore her when she tries to talk down her work. This woman can bake the hell out of a cake, I'm telling you."

Monroe nodded. "It's true. I'll probably never chew another bite of store-bought baked goods without not-so-secretly yearning for hers. She's really got a gift."

"Thank you," Wren replied, blushing. "Now, what kind of cake were you two looking for?"

"Andie insists that we don't want anything too fancy, but personally, I'd love a three-layer cake, with dark chocolate and raspberry, decorated to look like a bear."

"A bear?"

"It's an inside joke," Andie said, taking a photo of the lights down the street. Cat was staring at Monroe. "A really funny one."

"Sorry, do you two know each other or something?" Wren asked. Was this one of the old girlfriends Monroe had mentioned? An old flame? Her stomach sparked with jealousy.

"No, we've never met," Cat replied. "Which is honestly pretty surprising, given I have a feeling we share certain hobbies."

"Catriona," Andie called in a singsong voice, "you're the one who wanted to get the cake squared away. I told you I'd be happy with one from the freezer."

"Yes—anyway—Wren, would that be something you could do? We're looking at an early April date. Either the eighth or the tenth, depending on the venue."

Wren nodded. "Yes, I can do that."

"How much do you need for a deposit?"

"Oh, that's okay—"

"Half," Jaime interrupted. "She takes half for a deposit, and to secure the date."

Cat nodded. "Sure thing. Get us a price and we'll send it over first thing tomorrow."

"Should we take a look at the festival?" Andie suggested, snapping a few more photos. "The lighting is really gorgeous. I'm not usually one for portraits or still life, but there's some real potential here."

"Are you a professional photographer?" Wren asked.

"Wildlife, mostly." Andie looked sideways at Cat, who was lagging behind. "I caught a lucky break around this time last year, and I've spent all year traveling for a couple of weeks at a time, then coming home to edit and submit to various publications."

"That sounds so glamorous!"

"Trust me, when you're freezing your buns off in a snowy tent in Yellowstone, it doesn't feel at all glam. As much as I love it, I spend a lot of that time wishing I was home with Cat."

"I wish I had that. I mean—I have Jaime, and we're very close, but, you know. It's different."

"Are you and Monroe not...?" Andie asked.

"No."

"Huh. Thought I sensed a little something there. Maybe I'm wrong."

"I'm not so sure that she's interested in... that."

Andie pointed at the food stalls and gasped. "I've not had anything since lunch, and that all smells like heaven."

Jaime caught up to them, draping an arm over Wren's shoulder. "Am I finally getting to have a corndog, or will there be another bear sighting?"

"What?" Andie barked, whipping her head around. "What do you mean, bear sighting?"

"And I'd have thought a wildlife photographer would be used to that," Jaime said, laughing. "It was a joke. No bears in Roanoak Falls. Put your camera away. The only thing at the festival to take photos of is food and my borderline questionable fashion sense." They smirked. "The only wildlife here is probably a gaggle of raccoons sifting through someone's garbage. Or maybe Wren before she gets coffee in the morning."

Wren snorted and punched them in the arm. "Shut up." She pulled her cable-knit hat down around her ears. "Andie? You ready?"

Andie typed something on her phone before brightening. "Oh, you know me, always on the job. Let's get some grub."

Chapter 14

"So," Cat said, putting her phone back in her pocket. "You lived here long?"

"I don't live here, I'm just here on business," Monroe replied, far too aware of the mounting pile of missed calls that she still hadn't returned. Steve would probably blow a gasket soon. "It's a nice town, though."

"Are you feeling okay? You look a little... peaky."

"Peaky?"

"I know you don't know me, but I can tell that something is wrong. Has your shift pattern been off?"

Monroe's stomach clenched. "My work shifts are fairly flexible, except for meetings with city council and weekly—"

"Not work shifts," Cat said, her brows knit with concern. "You know. *Shifts.*"

"Listen, lady, I don't know who you think you are, but I have no idea what you're talking about. I met you less than five minutes ago and you're accusing me of being sick, or something."

Cat pulled her past the tree line. "You know, right? Like, you know what you are?"

"I'm a human," Monroe spat. "Now, if you'll excuse me, I need to get some food." She flinched at the vibrations at the base of her spine.

"It's starting already, isn't it? I can see it in your eyes."

"Get away from me."

"Just let me help!"

"I don't need any help."

"Okay," Cat said, releasing her grip. "Relax. I'm sorry that I scared you.

Why are you shifting so early? The full moon isn't for a couple more days."

Monroe jerked away, marching back towards the sidewalk. "I don't know what you're talking about," she said, but her voice was wavering. Did this woman know what she was? How? She had to get out of town, and fast, never mind Wren and Jaime. It was all a silly dream to think she could stay, anyhow.

"I'm the same as you," Cat called after her. "The same. I know you're in pain. Something is wrong, isn't it?"

She stopped in her tracks. "What do you mean *the same?*"

"I'm hardly going to shout it out, am I? Come back, let's talk."

"Alright," Monroe said when they were face-to-face once again. "Talk."

"I just texted Andie and said we might be awhile. She'll keep the others busy. They new friends of yours?"

"My job keeps me on the road."

"Is that on purpose?"

"More or less."

"When was your last shift?"

Monroe snapped the band at her wrist, willing the ache in her muscles to subside. "Prove to me that you are what you say you are."

"I can't. Not right now, anyway." Cat unlocked her phone, scrolling through photos. "Here. This is a photo Andie took last year. That's me," she said, pointing to a large bear, leaned against the thick trunk of a felled tree. "And that's my sister, the boys, and Dee."

"You're... all of you?"

"Yes." She scrolled past some more photos. "And here's another one we took just after we shifted back. Look at the time stamps if you don't believe me."

"I thought I was the only one."

"You've never met another Bear? What about your parents?"

"No."

"That's rough. When was your first?"

"Eleven," Monroe answered. "And my last shift was last night. Before that, two nights prior, and before *that*, almost a year."

"I'm sorry, I thought you said a year."

"I did. Late January last year."

Cat's eyes widened with surprise. "How are you doing that? And... why?"

"My parents took me to see a lot of specialists. I practice a lot of self control. As for why... why wouldn't I? You're telling me you enjoy feeling like your skin is being ripped apart?"

"It's not supposed to feel like that, Monroe. Our youngest Bear, Delilah, went a few months trying to stall, and she was in seriously rough shape when we found her. I can't even imagine the pain you go through."

"It's always felt like that for me."

"Have you ever allowed yourself to shift on a full moon? Not tried to fight it?"

"No. When I was young, I was usually taken for observation and they pumped me full of all sorts of things to keep the beast away."

"Did any of it work?"

Monroe sighed. "Not really. And now..." she trailed off, not sure if she should share more.

"And now what?"

"I'm not fully shifting back anymore."

"What?"

"I have... *fur*." She whispered the last word, ashamed. "On my side. I'm scared."

"Do your friends know?"

"Not about that, but they know the other part. Wren saw me, I got too hungry, and then I panicked, and... well, you know."

"I don't usually shift outside the usual lunar phase. You're having uncontrolled shifts because you're bottling it all up. It's not good for you."

"What, so you just... let it happen every month?"

Cat nodded. "Yes."

"What about Andie?"

"She knows. It's fine."

"Aren't you worried that you'll be hauled off for experiments? I don't ever want to see the inside of one of those hermetically sealed rooms again. Even the thought—" She flinched from the pulsating ache in her joints.

"We're careful. It's good to have people watch our backs. People like Andie. Or... Wren."

Monroe shook her head. "No. I don't want to put that on her. I don't want her getting all wrapped up in this, in my disease."

"It's not a disease."

"Might as well be."

"There's joy in it too, if you just allow yourself to let go a little," Cat countered. "I understand you're afraid, and I can't imagine not knowing my whole life that I wasn't the only one out there, but you can't carry on this way. It's going to destroy you."

"What do you know? You just let it happen to you, you give in and let it take over. How much of your life have you lost to losing control?"

"How much of yours have you wasted trying to rule over nature with white knuckles?"

"At least I *tried*."

Anger flashed across Cat's face. "I'm only trying to help."

"Your idea of help is to let it take over and put Wren in danger. Besides, I barely know her! No, thank you, I'll just do what I've always done."

"I don't think you realize what you're doing to yourself. If you don't start owning up to who and what you are, it's going to take over one day, and then what? It won't matter that you spent decades trying to force it down, it will be like that, forever."

Fear rippled along the base of Monroe's neck. "You don't know that."

"I do. I understand that until five minutes ago, you didn't know that you weren't the only one, but most of us grew up around others of our kind. Stories get told. Warnings get passed down."

"Maybe they're just that—stories."

"If that's a risk you're willing to take, then I can't stop you," Cat said, her tone barbed with frustration. "You should eat. I can already feel your shift just on the edge. It's like energy, crackling in the air. Can't you feel it?"

Monroe flinched again. "It only feels like pain." She snapped the band against her wrist. One, two, three, ten times, her eyes squeezed shut, her breath labored.

"Does that... help?" Cat asked, gesturing at the band on Monroe's wrist.

"Sometimes. Lately... not so much."

"What did Wren do when she saw you?"

"She brought me food. She stayed with me until it was over."

"Sounds like a good person."

"She is."

Cat sighed and leaned against a tree, her hands resting in the front pocket of her hoodie. "Jaime told us you're letting them stay with you. Hell of a thing for a stranger to offer, especially one hell bent on secrecy and hiding."

"I didn't want them to suffer. It's Christmas, after all."

"Still."

"I've spent most of my life alone." Monroe snapped the band four more times, focusing on the sharp sting against her skin. "It was impulsive, and I probably shouldn't have. Now they're dragged into my mess."

"I'll bet they prefer that over freezing in a cold house."

"I wouldn't be surprised if they both left in the morning."

"Monroe," Cat said, gently this time, "it is possible to find love of all kinds, you know. Even with people who aren't like us."

"Us."

"I know it probably still feels like a shock."

Tears pricked at Monroe's eyes. "I don't think I can even begin to process it."

"Food might help. I don't know about you, but I'm starved, and smelling those funnel cakes for the past twenty minutes is making me feel more bear than woman." Cat reached her hand out. "Come on, they're waiting for us."

"No, I think I should just go home. Tonight hasn't gone at all like I'd hoped."

"It will be easier if you just... if you just *listen* to me. I'm trying to help."

"Your way can't be the only right way. Allowing yourself to be ripped apart and reassembled every month? God, it would be even more exhausting than it already is! And to just—give in? No. I won't, I... I can't do that. No."

"I didn't expect to meet another Bear out here, but I did, and you're making it very difficult to help you."

"Then don't. Just leave me alone."

"You know what? Fine." Cat tossed a business card at her, and it landed in the snow. "My contact details are on there, if you ever decide to learn about how we live."

Monroe turned, leaving the card where it lay. "No thanks."

* * *

Monroe gripped the snow-covered tree, focusing on the frosty pain in her fingertips instead of the twisting ache in her stomach. What the hell did that woman know, anyway? It could all be a lie, a dangerously convincing fabrication to lead her straight into a trap.

Unlikely, though.

The truth was often difficult to pick out, especially in the history books she'd spent years poring over, looking for some sign that there were others. Myths, fairy tales, never anything concrete—the Bears had hidden themselves well. In plain sight, even as... whatever it was Cat did for a living. She hadn't asked.

Her fingers closed around the damp business card in her pocket. She'd gone back to get it after Cat had disappeared back into the crowd on Main Street, because her curiosity was always stronger than her resistance, even as a child. She took out the card to examine it in the faint light of the distant twinkling lights. There were teddy bears across the top and bottom, and contact details that included a hospital phone number. The other side read, *Catriona Evans, registered nurse.* Better to ask a nurse for help than someone else, maybe.

Throbbing with cold, she released the tree's bark, leaving two mottled handprints where the frost had melted. She ran hot, rarely feeling the cold, but it didn't prevent her skin from growing sensitive to the plummeting temperatures.

It had been years since the last glimmer of hope. She didn't even remember how to believe in something better, so long had she been resigned to the reality of what she was, swallowing it back, snapping thick yellow rubber bands against her wrist, fingernails digging into her own flesh for control.

She stepped out from the trees onto the sidewalk, the coarse salt crunching under her boots. The displays were brightly lit with colorful flood lamps. One was an ice sculpture of a hulking lumberer, a huge axe resting over her shoulder, her mouth set into a wide grin, a tribute to the town's lumbering history.

Everything in Roanoak Falls was almost annoyingly quaint, from the matching awnings emblazoned with the town's crest, a set of crossed axes, to the paved walkway through the display, lined at the borders with delicate wrought-iron fencing. It was a work of art in and of itself, a struggling town trying to pull itself up after their main industry went bust. Whoever worked on this event, planned it, decorated, they loved the place deeply, and it showed. The streets were crowded with people from nearby towns, maybe even from the city, they'd all driven all the way here just for the event.

She stepped up to the coffee kiosk, already deeply enamored with the rich scent of freshly ground beans. "A coffee, please," Monroe said, handing over a crisp five-dollar bill. "Keep the change."

"How do you want it?"

"Do you have anything sweet and seasonal?"

The barista grinned. "We have five. Hazelnut spice, eggnog cream, gingerbread—"

"The gingerbread, please."

"Whipped cream?"

Monroe nodded. "Please." She handed over another bill. "And one of those chocolate muffins."

"Sure thing, just be a minute."

The air was crisp in the way that your lungs felt awakened, alive with the zeal of early winter. It was infinitely preferable to the muggy oppression of summer, and Monroe breathed deep the soft, clean air that was never present in the cities. For the first time in all the hundreds of places she'd been, she didn't want to leave.

Her phone buzzed again. Steve. She couldn't ignore him forever, not if she wanted to keep her job. "Hello, Steve," she said, taking the coffee and the muffin from the barista. "What can I do for you?"

"Where the hell have you been, Chase? I've been calling you nonstop since last night!"

"Have you? My reception out here is terrible."

"You said you'd check in after the meeting, and then I get nothing but radio silence. What the hell are you playing at?"

She sat on a nearby bench, balancing the coffee on her knee. "What am *I* playing at? Explain to me why Marcie showed up down here, talking up the would-be mayor?"

"Come on, is that why you're mad? Corporate just wanted to make sure we're all on the same page, here. Many hands make light work, and all that. We just wanted to have all the bases covered, and besides, I did tell you that it was a possibility."

"That woman showed up at the meeting after Marcie was filling her ears with numbers, and she tanked the entire presentation. I'd have had them, Steve, but now—" She sighed. "Now I just don't know if I care anymore."

"Don't *care* anymore? That's hardly language I'd expect from regional manager material. Listen Chase, I'm going to give you one more chance to rectify this whole mess, alright? Catch the first flight out back here and we'll have a chat about how you can make this up to the company."

"I'm sorry?"

"Marcie will take things from there. From what she's told us, you've not been anywhere near city hall most days you've been down there. This isn't like you, but I have to say, I'm not impressed. We need to see some serious improvement if you're going to continue at this company."

"After being the most efficient in our department for nearly a decade? One failure and I'm on the rocks?"

"We expect excellence."

"Yet I know for a fact that Danny has missed every projection since he started... but I guess that's okay because he's your nephew."

"Excuse me?" Steve roared. "He's learning! He's working hard! But you—you're sabotaging the company with your laziness, your sheer contempt for this project, and I will not have it, Chase."

She took a bite of her muffin. "Okay. I quit." The words came far easier than she thought they would have.

"What?"

"I. Quit."

"Let's not be hasty here, Chase. There's no need for you to have some kind of breakdown over this. Come back to the office, we can talk about working this through, alright?"

"Nah."

"Do you realize what a lurch you're leaving us in, and right before this deadline? It's selfish! That woman isn't the only one running now, or haven't you heard? This deal isn't an easy win anymore with two mayoral candidates to cozy up to!"

Monroe sipped at her coffee. It was glorious, a rich roast, spiced ginger, and enough whipped cream to swim in. "Marcie can do it."

"You and I both know she's not a closer. *You're* my closer, Chase."

"Should have thought about that before you sent her down here. This is a special place, Steve. You can't just bulldoze over it like you have with all the others. In fact, I think the surveyors were wrong. A superstore doesn't belong in Roanoak Falls at all."

"This is a betrayal, Chase. If you really leave like this, I'm not writing you any reference letters, and anyone who calls will get an earful about what an unreliable, entitled—"

"I don't think a reference letter will be necessary."

"You can't live off of Christmas spirit, Chase. The mortgage still comes due at the end of the month."

"Steve, did you know that I don't even have my own place? I rent a crappy apartment back east that I'm rarely even able to stay in because you have me on the road all the time." She nibbled at the muffin, the deep chocolate and cherry taste awakening her taste buds and her appetite. "Good luck. I'm sure the local paper will be thrilled to know what you've all been up to."

"You signed a non-disclosure agreement."

"You're right, I did—but I'm sure one of their ambitious reporters will look into comparing results to promises made in nearby towns."

"I'll destroy any prospect of working in this industry again," he spat.

"Goodbye, Steve," she answered, ending the call. Finishing her muffin and every last crumb, she blocked his number and deleted the contact info for him and everyone else in Syndicorp. As she sipped at her coffee, savoring the silkiness of a beautifully crafted beverage, she felt a little bit freer.

A beaming grin spread across her face. She had to tell Wren.

Chapter 15

Jaime stole the last piece of funnel cake before Wren could slap them away. "Delicious."

"Hey!" Wren protested. "You already ate yours!"

"You were letting it get cold!"

"I was saving some for Monroe!"

"Don't bother," Cat said, sidling up next to Andie. "She went home."

"Went home? Why?"

Andie exchanged a look with her fiancée. "It didn't go well?"

"No. Not at all, in fact."

"You can't save them all, Catriona."

Cat huffed, the puff of breath from her mouth dissipating into the frosty air. "I know, but there aren't even that many of us left to save."

"What are you talking about?" Wren asked. "Is Monroe okay?"

"She won't be, if she keeps on with this path."

"...Syndicorp?" Jaime asked.

"I know that you both know she's..." Cat leaned in, her voice almost a whisper against the din of the festival, "a Bear. And so am I."

Jaime stared with wide eyes. "Are you joking me?"

"No. There's not many of us left, not in this country, anyway."

"You're telling me I somehow met two of you in the space of a week?"

"What are the odds?" Andie said, smiling. "Should we get some mulled wine?"

"Wait," Wren protested. "Why did Monroe leave?"

"She didn't like what I had to say," Cat answered.

"And what was that?"

"Just that she's hurting herself by forcing it down. It's unhealthy, and if she doesn't stop, it could have permanent effects. She's still taking it all in, I think."

"That makes two of us," Jaime said. "What, are vampires real, too?"

Cat made a face at them. "Don't be ridiculous. Of course not."

"Wolves? Were? Wolves?"

"There are those, yes. Other predators in other places, too, but we tend to keep to ourselves for the most part."

"I'll be damned," Jaime said. "It's not even the right season for this."

"What is that supposed to mean?"

"Seems more appropriate for Halloween."

Cat took a large bite of Andie's funnel cake, maintaining eye contact. "No. It isn't."

"We try to stay away from harmful stereotypes," Andie added. "Most weres are very conscious of their ecological and societal impact. Besides, Christmas is Cat's favorite holiday. Well, after Thanksgiving, anyway."

"Where did Monroe go?" Wren asked. "She shouldn't be alone right now."

"I don't know," Cat answered. "And I think maybe she does need some time alone, to think."

"And if she gets so upset that she shifts again?"

"She'll be fine. She headed off into the woods."

Wren covered her mouth with a gloved hand. "But the light walk is on the other side of those trees."

"Oh, shit," Cat replied. "I didn't know. We don't want to draw too much attention in case... well, in case. I hope I didn't upset her too much."

"I'll go."

"Wait—"

"Don't follow me. I'm going to go find her." Wren thrust the empty paper plate at Jaime. "If I don't text in thirty minutes, come looking."

She headed off into the trees, the light of the nearly full moon on such a cloudless night casting long shadows from each bare branch. It was cold, but clear, crisp without wind. "Monroe?" she called softly, looking for a sign of footsteps in the muddy undergrowth.

There was no sign of woman nor bear in the trees, no snapped branches, no prints, and no one to respond to her. This set of trees was shallow, less than one hundred feet in width, but dense. In the summer, when the limbs were laden with leaves, it was a popular spot for people to escape the persistent sunshine of Main Street.

"Monroe?" she said again, nearing the opposite edge of the tree line. From there, she could already see the sparkling of the lit walkways, with twinkling lights strung overhead, guiding people through the gentle maze of sculpted ice statues and festive displays, all dedicated to the town's history.

Wren peered through the crowd, worried that Monroe had torn off across the long, flat field into the reserve beyond again. Though they hadn't known each other long, she felt... responsible wasn't the right word, but maybe drawn to Monroe, despite everything—the bear was one thing. Syndicorp was another entirely.

"Wren! I was so hoping I'd see you here." Amber Pennington appeared from behind a display, predictably dressed in that year's high fashion, including brand new, unscuffed boots.

"Oh, hi, I was just looking—"

"For me? Oh, you're always so sweet. You really are a gem of this town, you know that? Everything got a little bit brighter when you showed up."

"That's very nice of you to say."

Amber reached out and tucked a stray hair back into Wren's braided crown. "It's the truth." She smiled, and in that light, she was pretty, a hint of playfulness in her rosy cheeks. "I didn't hear from you after our date the other night."

"I've been... busy."

"I wasn't sure if people still play by that three day rule, you know, texting before that looks a little desperate, or something?"

"I wouldn't ever call you desperate." Wren shoved her hands in her pockets to warm them. "Determined, maybe."

"Are you... here with someone?"

"Sort of. My friends are back on Main Street."

"Friends... plural?"

"Jaime, and..." Wren trailed off, unsure of how much to share. "A couple of visiting tourists who are getting married nearby in the spring. They've asked me to do their wedding cake."

"A wedding! Well, that's very exciting, isn't it? I don't know if I'd ever get married again. Maybe once was enough, you know?"

"They seem very happy together."

"And they're... paying you?"

Wren nodded. "Yes."

"Just be careful. I know not everyone has the right brain for business. It can be very easy to lose your way and end up in debt. I've seen it happen time and time again over the years, especially here."

"Oh, I don't know about all that, I'm still figuring things out."

"Good. Have you heard they say that ninety-five percent of small businesses fail in their first five years? Not a risk I'd want to take, that's for sure." Amber threw an arm around Wren's shoulders and pulled her closer. "Do you think your friends would mind if I stole you away? I've missed you the past few days."

"Oh, uh—"

"I know that Jaime doesn't like me, but it was nothing personal—I have to make a million tough decisions every day, and theirs was just one more on the pile."

"They understand," Wren lied, knowing full well that Jaime would nurse that grudge until their last breath. "How is the campaign going?"

"Swimmingly! I look forward to the vote next week. The sooner I'm in office, the sooner I can get Roanoak Falls back on track."

"Back on track?"

"People need jobs, Wren. Syndicorp is how we achieve that."

Wren pulled away. "No, I'm sorry, I disagree."

"Excuse me?" Anger flickered across Amber's face. "How can you possibly disagree?"

"They aren't good for towns like ours. There has to be another way, other than giving in and letting them walk all over us."

Amber laughed. "That just isn't how the world works. You can't magic up more funds for the public purse. You can't wish your way into prosperity. You have to make the hard choices, the difficult ones that other people are too cowardly to make."

"I guess that's why I'm not running for Mayor. I wouldn't want that weight on my shoulders."

"Oh, you," Amber said, softening. "You always know how to make me feel better. I bet if you met Marcie, you'd get on great. She's very enthusiastic about making this place as vibrant as it was thirty years ago."

"I hope that's true." Wren allowed her to wrap her arm around again, unsure of how to feel. "I know that I wasn't born here, but I love it. I don't want to see it become another carbon-copy ghost town with nothing other than those damned soulless super stores."

"I can promise you that won't happen. Don't you worry your pretty little face about it. Syndicorp isn't as bad as everyone says. Heck, even you were befriending that other one. What was her name again?"

"Monroe Chase. I've been staying at her rental after my heating broke."

"With a *stranger*? Lordy, Wren, you could have come and stayed with me!"

"It's worked out well. She's staying closer to Joe's, so I don't have as long a walk to get there."

"You really should learn to drive."

"I know how to drive, I just don't have a car."

"You're welcome to drive me around anytime, just say the word."

"I should probably get back to my friends, they'll be waiting for me."

Amber leaned down and kissed her. "I understand. I hope I'll see you soon."

"Uh, sure." Wren's head was swimming. When she turned to walk back to Jaime and the others, she saw Monroe staring at her from a park bench.

Chapter 16

Of course, Monroe thought bitterly. Why had she ever even entertained the idea of Wren, when there were other, more suitable and less monstrous women eagerly waiting to date her?

"I was looking for you," Wren said as she sat on the bench next to her. "We were worried."

You didn't look worried to me, is what Monroe wanted to say. "I'm sorry for worrying you," is what came out of her mouth. "You can go back to the others, I'm fine."

"Are you sure?"

"Positive." It was a lie, but maybe a convincing one. She'd calmed down after her call with Steve, but not enough to forgo worrying about another shift. "I just needed some fresh air and some quiet."

"I understand. Pretty wild stuff, huh?"

"Yep."

Wren reached out for her. "Are you upset?"

"No," Monroe replied, pulling away. Another lie, but one to protect herself. Admitting that she'd almost come to terms with asking for help, just to see Wren with Amber, might send her down a spiral she'd never escape from. "I told you, I'm fine."

"Do you want me to leave?"

"You can do whatever you want. It's a free country, so I'm told."

"If you don't want me here, then—"

"Go back to Amber, I'm sure she'd be more than happy to spend the evening with you." The words tumbled out of Monroe's mouth, barbed and laced with bitterness. "I'll be leaving town soon, anyway."

"I didn't mean for that to happen. I was out here looking for you!"

"And you found her instead. I get it. Trust me, I understand. This is a recurring theme in my story. Despite what anyone says, no one really wants to spend time with a beast."

"You're not a beast."

"I am, in fact. A grotesque, dangerous monster who never should have made it this far in the first place." Her face flushed, her jaw clenched firm. "Just go, Wren. I'll see you back at the house, alright? It's fine. It's not your fault, and I don't blame you. This is just how things are."

"If you would crawl out of that hole of self-pity, maybe you could shut up and listen for once!" Wren shot back, her voice tight with emotion. "I like being around you. Your... condition... is part of who you are and it's what makes you you. How could you ever think that I'd be so shallow as to write you off for that? I haven't walked away yet. Why would I now?"

"Self-pity?" Monroe repeated. "You think this is about self-pity?"

"You're so wrapped up in the past that you can't see what's going on in the present. There are four people at this festival willing to be your friend, if you'd just let us in."

"Maybe friendship isn't what I wanted!"

Wren jerked away. "What do you mean?"

"Nothing." Monroe smoothed her hair back, closing her eyes to the twinkling lights with a deep breath. "I'll be fine, Wren, and you can tell the others that, too."

"Tell me what you meant."

"Why?"

"Because... because I want to know!"

Monroe gave a bitter laugh. "So you can laugh with Amber about how someone as horrendous as me wanted to spend time with you?"

"No, that's not—"

"You can sit around, chuckling at the desperate, foolish, unemployed—"

"What? What do you mean, unemployed?"

"Nothing. I was just using hyperbole."

"No, you weren't, I can tell. What's going on, Monroe?"

"Just leave it alone, okay? I see where everyone stands now, and I'll be out of your hair soon enough. You won't have to worry about me losing my control ever again, and you can pretend this never happened. Hell, write a book about it. I'm sure it will sell millions of copies."

"Or, and this is just a suggestion, we just take a breath to have a calm discussion? Your pupils are huge, and I imagine that's not a great sign," Wren said, her brow furrowed with worry.

"You let me worry about my pupils."

"I'd rather you didn't worry at all, truth be told."

Monroe sighed. "I don't think that's ever going to be in the cards for me. Life just doesn't work like that. Not for me."

"Maybe that's because you're too stubborn to see any other reality than the one you've crafted in your head. People care about you. *I* care about you."

"Not the way that I—Wren, I understand why you'd choose someone like Amber Pennington. She's gorgeous, she's rich—"

"I could say the same thing about you."

"—and she's not a monster."

"Neither are you."

"I need you to stop, Wren. I can't handle hearing these things, it gives me false hope that—"

"False?" Wren whispered. "It's not false."

"But—"

"Honestly, Monroe, you're the most stubborn woman I've ever met. It's like you flat out refuse to see what's right in front of you."

"I saw you kiss her."

"I would have rathered it was you." Wren leaned forward and their lips met, warm and soft, like sparks of electricity sending heat across every nerve.

Monroe couldn't resist it, despite knowing this would only make it more painful when she was left alone again. She pulled Wren closer, deepening their kiss, the taste of gingerbread and cherry chocolate mingling with the powdered sweetness of funnel cake.

It began to snow, with huge, fluffy flakes landing in Wren's hair like sparkling confetti, and on her cheeks like wintery freckles. It was everything, all at once, the distant sounds of the crowds drifting into the background until it was just the two of them, wrapped in a kiss, bathed in the warm light of the tiny bulbs that hung over their heads, strung high over the path between hulking conifers.

"You're beautiful," Monroe uttered, and the truth was so sharp it cut into her like a knife, slicing through the stoney exterior she'd spent a lifetime building. "Snow suits you."

"I always did like the cold. It's why I moved here in the first place."

"I... don't know what to say."

Wren put her mittened hand in Monroe's. "Say you won't leave. At least, not yet. Stay until Christmas. I'm sure you can give you boss some excuse—"

"I quit."

"You what?"

"Quit." Monroe gave her a half smile. "It wasn't for me anymore."

"That's... wow. I can't believe it."

"You were right. They do take everything they can. I know I have a lot to make up for, not that it will help the places that have already been steamrolled."

Wren flung her arms around Monroe. "Does this mean you'll stay?"

"For now, I guess. Until—" *Until things inevitably fall apart*, she wanted to say. "Until the new year."

"I'll take that. A lot can change in a few weeks."

"Did you hear that Amber has a competitor for the mayor's seat?"

Wren gasped. "What? No!" She snorted. "She's going to be *pissed*."

"That's for damn sure."

"Who is it?"

"I don't know, I only found out about it as I was telling my boss where he can shove it."

"Did you really say that?"

Monroe laughed. "No. But I should have. Jerk."

"I bet we can find out at city hall tomorrow. What do you think? I work opening but I'm off by two." Wren laid her head on Monroe's shoulder. "Or do you have plans, now that you're a free woman, unencumbered by corporate interests?"

"Two works. I've always been an early riser, but I'm sure I can make myself busy. I have a few ideas of how to fill my time."

"Oh yeah? And what's that?"

"Don't be nosy."

"Always the secrets with you."

"Only until I figure a few things out, alright?" Monroe kissed her again, drawn in by Wren's plump, kissable lips. "I promise."

"Hmm. Fine. You're always a mystery, aren't you?"

"I've had a lifetime of practice."

"Cat wants to help, you know."

"I know."

"I think you should let her." Wren grabbed the coffee and took a swig. "That's really good. Gives me an idea, actually."

"Always with the creative brain, you are."

"What, you never wake up in the middle of the night absolutely possessed by an idea you just have to try out right then?"

Monroe smirked. "No. I like charts and data. The most creative I am is deciding what color to make the graph lines in the presentations. I use purple if I'm feeling spicy."

"Whoa, easy there, tiger. Purple graphs? Someone better rein you in before you *really* get wild."

"I know, next thing you know I'll be using *orange*." Monroe took the cup back and drained the last of it. "And I will let her. It's just... it's a lot, and all at once. It's like a dam breaking, and I'm afraid I'll drown."

Wren pressed her cheek to Monroe's. "I won't let you drown. I promise."

Chapter 17

"Good morning, Mr. Ranelli," Wren chirped, wiping her boots at the door.

"I have a favor to ask," he replied, frowning at the stack of leaflets that Amber had left at the register.

"Sure thing, what's up?"

"Throw these away."

"She'll just drop off more, you know. She's persistent."

"I don't think she will once she hears from city hall this morning."

Wren took the pamphlets. "Oh?"

"Haven't you heard? I'm running for mayor."

"Oh! Wow, I... I didn't expect that."

"No? You're the one who inspired me. You said I should run, so... I am." He looked up from the counter, his face set and determined. "Something in this town isn't right. I'd say something smells fishy but we're a hundred miles from the nearest lake."

"Something is rotten in Denmark?"

He laughed. "That's even further."

"What's fishy, then?"

"I don't quite know. I asked that young reporter they've got at the local, the one who's fresh out of college, to look into it. I don't know if there's anything to find, but if there is..."

"Anything like what?"

"There's too many of these Syndicorp people slithering around. First one, and then another?" He shook his head. "No, I'm not going to stand for it. You know what will happen if they get a foothold here."

Wren nodded. "I do."

"We'll both be out of jobs." He sighed, punching a number into the register. "Things are hard enough as it is. We don't need any more challenges. I'm tired of letting life happen to me. I'm taking a stand."

"Good for you."

"I'm not going to ask you to help me, but—"

"I'll help."

"—I was going to ask if that friend of yours is free to do some consulting for me. I know it's last minute, given the vote is in just a few days, but I could use some guidance. I've never done this before."

"I'm sure Jaime would be more than happy to lend a hand," Wren replied, already sending a text. "Anything has to be better than just letting Syndicorp steamroll Roanoak Falls."

"I probably don't have a snowball's chance in hell of winning this thing, not when she makes the rounds at every PTA meeting, and bulldozes into every festival planning committee to crown herself queen of this place." He ran his hands over the old, cracked counter top. "But I have to try."

Wren's phone buzzed. "Jaime said they'd be right over to discuss campaign strategy."

"You're a useful woman to know, Wren Jackson."

"I do try to be useful. Most of the time, anyway."

The bells on the door jingled. "Joseph Ranelli, what the hell do you think you're doing?" Amber barked, not even stopping to wipe the wintery sludge from her boots as she stomped over the threshold. "Mutiny? Really?"

He blinked. "I don't think it's mutiny, unless you're on a boat."

"Oh, aren't we? I thought we were on the S.S. Screw Amber Over. Is that not the case?"

"It's not about that, it's about doing what's best for the town."

"I don't believe that for a second. You're trying to play this trashy altruistic angle, but I see right through you, old man."

"You should leave," he replied, his expression hardening. "We can discuss this at a later date, assuming you can do so in a civil manner."

"Civil? You want me to be civil? Fine, I'll be civil—let's discuss why you decided to hide the fact that you decided to run against me. Explain that. Go ahead, I'll wait."

"I think that uncontested elections are a farce. At least now, people will have a choice."

"And you think they'll pick you?" Amber asked with a snort. "You might have one of the oldest storefronts in town, but that doesn't mean that people will tick the box next to your name. It's a total waste of time."

He tilted his head gently. "If it's a waste of time, why are you so angry?"

"Because you didn't tell me! That's... breach of privacy, or something!"

"Mrs. Pennington, I do think it's best if you go. We aren't going to achieve anything here."

Amber gave him a broad smile. "That's not mayoral behavior, now is it? Roanoak Falls needs a leader that's willing to do the hard work of keeping this place together. Not you, me."

"I can appreciate that you are upset, but invading my place of work is highly unprofessional, and you know it."

She whirled on Wren, who was still holding the pamphlets. "Oh, Wren! I didn't know that you worked this morning, and look at you, ready to hand out my campaign materials."

"Something like that?"

"You're such a doll, an angel, in fact, and I don't know how bland this place would be without you in it. You deserve to work someplace better than in this dump, that's for sure."

"Uh—"

"Yes, well, we weren't all born into money, now were we?" Mr. Ranelli interrupted.

Amber sniffed. "I've worked hard my entire life, I'll have you know."

"Haven't we all? Yet you're living in that enormous house, and some people can't even make rent." He shook his head. "When I inherited this business, I also inherited all of its debt. It was about to go under when my father died fifteen years ago."

"Sounds like a bad investment to me."

"Some things are more important than investments." He gestured towards the door. "I have a meeting with my campaign manager, if you don't mind. May the best person win."

"Oh, I plan to," Amber hissed as she whirled out of the store. "You can bet this horrible little store on it."

"That may very well be the case," Mr. Ranelli mumbled, long after she was out of earshot.

"So what now?" Wren asked.

"First things first," Jaime announced, swanning in through the front door. "I've designed you a logo and a slogan. They're rudimentary, we're working on a tight schedule."

"Ranelli Cares," Wren read out from the mocked up sign in Jaime's hand. "I like it."

"I've already sent the mockup to the printers in town, I hope it's okay that I took the liberty to do that. Do you hate it?" they asked. "If you hate it, tell me now so I can call them."

Even the thick mustache couldn't hide Mr. Ranelli's smile. "I don't hate it. I don't know how you did that so quickly, though."

"I had a few ideas waiting for the right candidate." Jaime held out their hand. "Sir, it looks like that's you."

Mr. Ranelli shook their hand. "I suppose we should hand out some leaflets to folks, let them know my name will be on the ballot."

"Wren and Monroe can take the west end of town, I'll get north, and our new friends will get the light speed Roanoak Falls initiation by taking south and east. Fewer houses out that way."

"Do you think we can pull this off?" Wren asked. "Amber has been making inroads for this for years. I'm surprised she didn't throw a party when the last mayor retired."

Jaime smirked. "Amber might have the PTA on lock, but only out of fear. No one dares oppose her there, but we have everything else up for grabs. This shop has been here as long as most people can remember. It's one of the town's mainstays."

"I think we might have a chance," Mr. Ranelli said, tucking in his shirt. "But we need to do something big. Something people will remember."

"I have an idea," Wren said, "but we're going to need lots of eggs."

* * *

The sink was piled high with dishes, but Wren gave a satisfied sigh, wiping her hands on her striped apron. "That's all of them."

"How many now?" Monroe asked, already scrubbing one of the bowls.

"Five hundred even."

"I didn't even think that many people lived in Roanoak Falls," Jaime said, running a finger along a bowl and dripping the loose icing into their mouth.

"Don't be ridiculous, you know it's more than that," Wren replied with a laugh. "That first batch is done setting. Why don't you make yourself useful and start wrapping them up?"

"I bet there are faster ways to do this."

"Yes, in a professional kitchen there would be, but I don't have one of those just hanging around, now do I? Get wrapping, or we're going to be here all night."

Jaime held one up to the light, the perfect icing letters spelling out the campaign slogan glistening with the glitter dust. "I don't know how you got them all to look so perfect. Almost seems like a shame to give them to people to eat."

"They'll have a better impact than threats of influence. Flies and honey, goes the saying," Monroe interjected, elbow deep in steaming dish water. "It's the first rule of site acquisition. Tell everyone all the great stuff they'll get. Save the threats for the holdouts."

"And just when I thought I couldn't hate Syndicorp more," Wren said, "you come out with that."

Jaime wrapped the cookie in cellophane. "We have an insider perspective now, though. Might be useful if Amber *does* win."

"If you'd asked me even a month ago if I'd be this involved in a local mayoral election, I'd have laughed in your face." Wren laughed, wiping stray flour from the counter into her palm. "Probably even weirder for you, Monroe, right?"

"Hmm." Monroe slid another dish into the rack, but said nothing more as she plunged her hands back into the water.

"What does *that* mean?"

"I don't know if I should tell you or not. It might... change your opinion of me, in a negative way."

"Did you kill off the dissenters?" Jaime asked with a snort.

"No, I didn't kill anyone. Once you put it that way, giving out bribes almost seems tame in comparison."

Wren dusted her hands off over the garbage can, sending a flurry of floury flakes into the air. "Wait, what do you mean, bribes?"

"Oh, you know." Monroe shrugged, still facing the sink. "A few investments here, some community resource promises there, greasing the palms of the city hall and mayors always goes a long way to soften the blow."

"Did anyone ever refuse it?" Jaime asked.

Monroe laughed. "No. Not once."

"A rousing endorsement for local government, that's for sure," Wren said bitterly. "Nothing says community more than screwing over your neighbors for a little extra cash."

"Sometimes a lot of extra cash, depending on the scenario."

"How did you sleep at night?"

"I didn't," Monroe said, scrubbing egg yolk from a fork. "I never once felt good about it."

Jaime wrapped another cookie, tying a ribbon around it. "Then how come you never left?"

"It can be very hard to break a cycle once you're inside of it. Reaching for something new is sometimes so scary and overwhelming, you end up not reaching for anything at all."

"That's the saddest thing I've ever heard, and I've read a lot of indie poetry."

"What did you want to reach for?" Wren asked. "What was it that you were too scared to try?"

Monroe groaned, setting a measure cup upside down to drain. "You're going to laugh."

"We promise we won't laugh."

"I always wanted a quieter life. I want... I want friends, and backyard barbecues, and trips to the beach in the summer, and games nights, and a bowling league. I want the stuff I grew up seeing on tv."

"I take it back. That's the saddest thing I've ever heard," Jaime said. "Listen, I can't promise trips to the beach, I'm basically a vampire, but if you want a friend, you've got one." They set a full box of wrapped cookies aside. "I'm a terrible bowler, too."

Monroe sniffed and wiped at her face with the elbow of her sleeve. "I've never been bowling."

"Are you *crying*, Chase? Don't cry, it's just bowling, I—" Jaime pulled a phone from their pocket, interrupting themself. "Cat and Andie just texted that they finished wrapping their batch. How the hell did they do that so quickly?"

"Probably because they're actually wrapping and not yapping," Wren said, already setting aside her tenth completed cookie.

"They're coming to collect more."

"Good, we'll need the help at the glacial pace you're going." Wren cast a worried glance at Monroe, who was still finishing up the dishes. "Hey, I can do that if you need to go lay down."

Monroe shook her head. "Absolutely not. I said I would help, so I'm helping. It's not like I have anything else to do."

"Did your boss—er, ex-boss—ever stop calling?"

"No idea. I blocked the number. Blocked Marcie's, too, not that she tried calling me, anyway. Snake."

"Sounds like she was gunning for your job," Jaime said.

"She can have it. Best of luck to her."

Wren wrapped another cookie. "Don't wish her too much luck, we still want to have a fighting chance of beating this." She sighed, stretching her neck from side to side to ease the dull throb of the muscle ache. "I still can't believe you actually quit."

"It was a long time coming, I suppose. There's only so long you can just let life drag you along, drifting in the current, before something has to snap."

She pulled the plug on the sink and began to dry the dishes in the rack. "I'm still coming to terms with it, truth be told."

"That's understandable."

"A new beginning." Monroe sighed. "Whatever that might be."

Chapter 18

"I'll take it," Monroe said, looking around at the almost derelict building. "It has... potential."

"Do you need to speak to our mortgage lender? He's very good," the real estate agent replied, typing notes into her phone. "I can guarantee he'll get you something with a low rate."

"No, thank you. I'll be paying cash."

"I'll inform the sellers. Did you want to look around one last time?"

"I think we covered everything."

The agent gave her a broad, toothy smile. "Great! I'll get started on the paperwork, and if you pop into the office tomorrow before noon, we'll get this all cleared up before the office empties out over the holidays."

"Thank you, you've been very helpful."

"It was nothing! You're like a dream client." She flipped a business card out of her bag. "My cell, in case you need me for anything."

Monroe nodded. "Great." She looked up at the trees, the empty branches still despite the slight breeze. "I'm going to take some notes before I head off, get an idea of renovations."

"Take your time! I'll see you tomorrow." The agent got into her car, the engine so whisper quiet it could barely be heard as it backed out onto the street.

It wasn't much, but it was a start. A beginning, maybe. Or an end, if things didn't go as she hoped they would. She was coming to learn that anything was possible, good or bad. Turning her face towards the bright winter sky, she inhaled deep the crisp midwestern air. There was never air like that in the city, and she'd been in dozens of cities across the country and the world.

"Chase!"

Her stomach clenched even before she turned around. "Steve." Her shoulders tensed, sending a jolt of pain down her spine. "What are you doing here?"

"What am I *doing* here? Because of you, I had to fly halfway across the damned country to try to salvage this deal that you made such a mess of!"

"How did you find me?"

"It's not a big place, Chase. I kept driving around until I saw your rental car. The rental car that Syndicorp is paying for, or do I have to remind you?"

"Here," she said, tossing the key. "Take it."

"I'm not here for the key," he spat, tossing it back. "I don't know what's going on with this little breakdown you're having, but—"

"Little breakdown?"

"Listen, we all have those days, Chase. You just need a couple weeks off and you'll be right as rain. You're lucky I didn't report your resignation up the chain of command already."

"I'm not coming back."

He narrowed his eyes. "Look at this place. It's a dump. You're telling me this is your new dream? Poverty in some backwater?"

"A dump for now, maybe." She shoved her hands into her pockets. "What about Marcie? Have you been to see her yet?"

"I don't give a rat's ass about Marcie. She's not my closer. You are."

"Should have thought of that before you sent her down here to undermine me, then."

Steve gave her an exasperated sigh, his open coat blowing in the wind. "Is that what this is all about? Are you jealous that I sent her in? This is about teamwork, Chase, and—"

"It's not just about that. It's not really about that at all, it was just the catalyst I needed to get out."

"Syndicorp will end up in this town, you know. It's… inevitable. Doesn't it seem like a better plan to be on the winning team, rather than the losing one?"

"Sometimes you realize the team you've been playing for bought the referees."

"That's good, though. Then you win, and you keep on winning."

"Might win, but can't sleep at night. Not really."

"What is it you want in order to come back? A raise? We can give you a raise. More vacation time? Nicer rentals when you're on the road? What?"

Monroe shook her head. "It's not about any of those things. What I've been searching for, Syndicorp could never give. It can't."

"You're throwing away a lifetime of opportunities."

"Maybe so, but I'm happy taking that risk."

"This is your last chance to wise up, Chase, I mean it."

She nodded. "I understand. My decision is final."

"There's no coming back from this. You do realize that, right?"

"I do."

"Then as of right now, your employment with Syndicorp is terminated." His face hardened. "Don't ever ask me for a reference, Chase. You won't like how that ends."

"Noted."

"It doesn't matter what you think you're going to pull, here, two new superstores will be going up by the end of next year. There's nothing you can do to stop it, not even with this little tantrum you're having."

"Goodbye, Steve. And tell Marcie I said hello."

* * *

"That's the last house," Wren said, shoving the few remaining flyers into her bag. "I'm freezing."

"Here," Monroe said, draping her own thick pea coat over Wren's shoulders. "That should help until we get back."

"Won't you get cold?"

The frozen white light of the almost-full moon made even the week-old snow sparkle. "Nah. I'll be fine."

"Thank you for coming with me tonight."

"You know what they say, many hands make light work, or whatever."

"Still, you came here trying to turn Roanoak Falls into the next superstore location, and a week later you're volunteering for the opposition." Wren laughed, kicking her boot at some loose clumps of ice on the sidewalk. "Where did you go this morning, anyway?"

"Nowhere special," Monroe lied. She didn't want to scare Wren away, or snap the tenuous thread of connection by pouring out too much, too soon. "Just for a drive. Ran into my boss. Well, ex-boss now. I was formally terminated."

"I'm sorry."

Monroe laughed. "No you aren't. I bet you're thrilled that I left."

"I am pretty thrilled, I won't lie." Wren wrapped her mittened hand in Monroe's and sighed. "This feels good."

"It does."

"How does so much change in so short a time?"

"I guess life can do that, sometimes." Monroe hadn't even really begun to process how much had changed. It would take months, maybe even years, to unpack what had happened. "I'm glad it did, though."

"Me, too." Wren shivered, even beneath the weight of both heavy coats.

"We're almost home. I'll make some tea."

"How about hot chocolate? I think Jaime brought marshmallows back. They're out tonight, meeting with some friends a few towns over."

"Hot chocolate sounds nice." She eased open the front gate, the hinge giving a slight creak. Wren waited as she unlocked the door and pushed it open, feeling the wave of warmth rush out into the cold.

"I guess the vote is tomorrow," Wren said, slipping off her boots. "And the full moon."

"Big day for everyone." Monroe pulled her into a tight embrace. "Let's get you warmed up."

Wren snuggled into her arms. "How are you so warm?"

"It's the lunar cycle. I always run hotter around it. Always hungrier too."

"Are you scared about tomorrow?"

"The vote?"

"The moon."

Monroe sighed. "I don't want to think about it."

"Then we don't have to." Wren played with the hem of Monroe's shirt, face buried in her blazer.

Monroe jerked away. "Don't."

"What's wrong?"

"Just... don't."

"Am I misreading things here?" Wren asked, staring at the ceiling. "I thought... I thought that we were okay, and—"

"It's not you."

"What, '*it's not you, it's me,*' is that it?"

"No—no, it's not that. I like you a lot, maybe even—but I don't think you want to know me, not really. Not like that."

"I can assure you that I do."

"What?"

Wren's gaze fell on Monroe's face. "I do. Want to know you like that." She approached again, slowly this time, shrugging off both coats so that they fell to the floor with a quiet rustle. "Ever since I saw you in the store for the first time."

"Me being a beast doesn't change that?"

"You're not a beast, Monroe. You're a Bear. And you're beautiful." Wren leaned in for a kiss, wrapping her arms around Monroe and pulling her close.

Monroe sank into the kiss, forgetting everything else: the vote, her job, the moon, all of it. There was only her, and Wren, and the increasingly dizzying, overpowering emotion of the kiss. She gently pressed Wren against the wall, hungry for her touch, desperate for skin on skin, her warm hands now pressed against Wren's chilly hips. "Let's warm you up," she said again, with a growl to her voice.

Wren moaned softly. "Yes, please," and the sound of it sent heat shooting down between Monroe's thighs.

Wren's hands in her hair, pulling it out of the looped ponytail so that the dark hair fell around her shoulders. Wren's hands tugging at her belt loops, pulling her closer, the deep, tempting her to give in to the unspeakable need that was growing between them.

Monroe tugged at the waistband of Wren's fleece tights, reaching back to grab a fistful of flesh that made her breath catch short.

The house was silent except for the sound of their kisses, some sweet, some lingering with desire, but when Wren reached up Monroe's shirt, she pulled away again.

"What is it?" Wren asked, her voice a husky whisper.

"It's embarrassing."

"Whatever it is, I won't laugh or be afraid."

"I don't think that's possible," Monroe said, her eyes squeezed shut. "Please don't run away when you see it."

Wren unbuttoned the shirt, but didn't react at the odd trail of dark fur across the side of Monroe's ribcage. "Is this it? Some fur?"

"It's not normal."

"Almost everyone has fur." Wren pulled her own sweater off over her head, holding her arms aloft. "See?" she said with a light laugh that sounded like stones skipping across placid water. "I have some, too." An eyebrow raised, a smirk playing on her lips, she was showing off the patches of hair under her arms. "No big deal."

"How are you so cute?"

Wren pulled her up the stairs with tempting kisses and gentle tugs at the hem of her shirt until they both fell into the unmade bed, a tangle of sheets and blankets that was warm and inviting for bare skin.

Clothes were taken off and dropped unceremoniously across the hardwood floor and over the wide rug that peeked out from beneath the bed. Monroe pulled the sheets and blankets over them, and she leaned over Wren, memorizing the way her face looked in the darkness, nothing but profile and shadows, hinting at what she looked like in daylight.

She kissed down Wren's neck and across her collar bone, her hands grasping at hips and thighs. "I've never wanted anyone so much," Monroe uttered, pausing at the crease where thigh met a thicket of hair.

"Then have me," Wren replied, her fingers entwined in Monroe's hair, pulling her in, gasping.

Soft and velvety, Monroe was lost in the moment where nothing else existed. She almost couldn't handle the pure, unadulterated brightness of it, the deep and unfiltered joy that was exploding from her every cell with every kiss, every whisper, every moan and breathless wish with the accelerating rhythm of the quiet dance until Wren cried out, gasping. She wound her fingers through Monroe's loose hair, pulling her in closer for another kiss, pulling her down and pressed against her before she rolled onto her side and straddled Monroe, running her hands over smooth skin and coarse fur.

"What now?" Monroe asked, tentative and nervous.

"Now, you let me return the favor," Wren replied, her hands flat against Monroe's thighs. "You are everything," she said, bending to plant kisses across Monroe's stomach, "and I'm never letting you go."

Monroe couldn't help the soft whimper that escaped her lips when Wren began, nor could she help how soon she reached the peak, muffling her voice with the back of her hand.

They held each other wordlessly. Monroe was memorizing every curve and angle of Wren's face in the dim light, every gentle shadow and crease, until they were both fast asleep in each other's arms.

Chapter 19

Wren perched on top of the counter, mug in her hands, the hot liquid warming her skin. It was a quiet morning, and she was basking in the early light of the day. There was nothing in the forecast other than sunny skies, perfect for a full moon.

The front door swung open and Jaime tumbled in, their expression almost giddy with anticipation. "I'm so glad you're awake. Have you seen the front page of the paper?"

"No, I only got up twenty minutes ago."

"Here." Jaime tossed a rolled up paper at her as they hung their coat on the hook. "Why are your coats on the floor?"

Wren tried to give a neutral stare, but her face betrayed her, cracking a smile. "No reason."

"*Well* then," Jaime said, an eyebrow raised as they hung up the other coats. "It's about damn time."

"It's been like, a week."

"Still. Come on, the paper! I've been absolutely busting to tell you since I picked up a copy on my way back this morning."

"You were out late."

"Fell asleep on their couch after I ate too much. Food coma. The *paper*, Wren!"

"Alright, alright!" She unfurled the paper and gasped. "Amber Pennington was taking *bribes*?"

"Are you even that surprised?"

"I mean... a little, yeah. She already lives in a huge house. What does she need bribe money for?"

"More designer suits?" Jaime mused, sitting on a stool at the counter and snatching a leftover muffin. "If we'd known this was going to break on voting day, maybe you wouldn't have had to make all those cookies."

"You never know who isn't going to read the paper before they go vote. I wonder if Mr. Ranelli knows."

"I texted him already."

"Wow, you work fast."

"I'm the campaign manager! It's my job!"

Wren skimmed the article. "What did he say?"

"Just that he hopes people vote for a better future. He was half-asleep, though."

"Crap, I have to open the store today, I totally forgot."

"Morning," Monroe said from the stairs, yawning. "I'll drive you. No sense waiting on a bus when I don't have anything better to do." She stretched her arms over her head. "What's the news?"

"Amber taking bribes from Syndicorp," Jaime answered. "Though we wouldn't have known exactly where to look without your help."

"I'm glad it led to some good, I guess. Though I strongly suspect the local paper will have Syndicorp's lawyers already ringing the phones off the hook. I bet they'll demand a retraction."

"Still, it's good this got out on the day of the vote, rather than the day after."

"Do you think it will affect turnout?" Wren asked, topping up her coffee.

Jaime folded the muffin wrapper neatly, creasing the edges. "Probably. Hopefully it helps us, instead of hurting us."

"What will happen if she wins, anyway?"

"We're screwed."

"We could always move," Wren said. "Monroe? Coffee?"

Monroe nodded. "Yes, please. And if I were you, I wouldn't want to move. It's... nice, here."

"I don't want to move, but who knows how bad things will get if Amber still wins. She'll probably sign everything over to Syndicorp before an official investigation is even launched."

"And Syndicorp will tie Roanoak Falls up with legal documents and court cases until the town's coffers are dry," Monroe added. "But let's not get ahead of ourselves—she might not win."

Wren hopped off the counter. "Jaime, do you need a ride to the store?"

"Nah," they said, draining their mug. "I need a shower and a change of clothes before I head over. You two go ahead."

"Shall we?" Monroe asked, gesturing towards the door.

"Thank you. I didn't feel like walking to the bus stop today. It's cold and I'm…" Wren trailed off as Monroe approached. "…tired."

"A good tired, I hope?"

"The best."

"Do you need anything while you're at work? Lunch? I can bring you lunch from that nice deli across town."

"You don't have to do that."

Monroe leaned in and kissed her, a delicate brush of the lips but enough to scramble Wren's thoughts. "But I want to. Besides, anything to make me forget about later."

"Are you going to be okay? Should I come with you?" Wren asked, zipping up her thick parka. "Snacks? Guard duty?"

"No," Monroe said, shaking her head. "Cat wants me to go out with her to some thick woods about fifteen miles from here. Dense, and a large reserve that's protected, so we'd be unlikely to run into anyone."

"Are you going to go with her?"

"I am, yeah. I figure… doing what I've done thus far hasn't really worked. It might be time to try something new."

Wren tried to ignore the dull spark of jealousy flickering at the edges of her mind. "Would you prefer to be with another Bear?"

"Absolutely not," Monroe said, pulling her in for another kiss. "Besides, I don't think I'm Cat's type." Locking the door behind them, she unlocked the rental. "I need to turn this one back in today, now that I'm officially no longer employed. I already extended the house through the new year, though."

"Do you regret it?"

Monroe thought for a moment as she started the car. "No."

"Not even a little?"

"The pay was decent, but what good is money if you aren't doing anything with it?"

"I don't know, I'll let you know if I ever get the opportunity," Wren replied with a laugh.

"Can I show you something real quick? I know you have to get to work. It won't take long. Five minutes."

"If it's the giant donut statue on the highway, I've seen it already. Jaime makes us take pictures next to it every year."

"There's a giant donut statue?"

"Definitely the most exciting thing about Roanoak Falls."

"Okay, well, no, it's not the giant donut statue. In fact, it doesn't look like much of anything right now."

Wren raised an eyebrow. "That's intriguing."

"It's right around the corner." Monroe pulled the car onto Main Street and parked in the small lot. "That building across the street."

"What about it? It used to be a small burger place. It closed when the owner died last year. You gonna tell me it's haunted, or something?"

"It's yours."

Wren laughed. "What do you mean, it's mine?"

"I mean, it's yours." Monroe leaned over and pulled some papers from the glove box. "Signed, sealed, and delivered."

Tears sprang to Wren's eyes. "What?" she said again, this time her voice barely above a whisper.

"I'm your first investor. The place is yours, and there's budget set aside for whatever you need to make it the bakery of your dreams."

"Is this a joke?"

"It is not a joke." Monroe opened her door. "Do you want to take a look?"

"Yes." Her boots crunched against the iced-over snow as she crossed the street, laying her palm flat against the front window. "How did you know? How did you know that this was the place?"

"Jaime might have mentioned it."

Tears sprang to Wren's eyes. "This can't be real. You barely know me, and this—this is the biggest thing anyone has ever done for me."

"I know you well enough to know that your skills are top notch. I might know someone to help with the business end of things... that is, if you're hiring."

"You're staying?"

Monroe shrugged. "As long as you'll have me."

"Can we go inside?" Too much emotion was welling up inside her; it was threatening to spill out at any moment.

"Sure." Monroe unlocked the door and then handed the key to Wren. "It's yours."

"It's..." she trailed off, overwhelmed. It was everything. It was years of potential, waiting to be engaged. The tables were caked with dust, the counters needed to be replaced, but... it was hers. It was the start of a dream coming true. It was early mornings quietly baking, and finally being able to build a life that she had wanted for so long. "It's perfect."

"It's ready for you to get started, whenever you're ready. I'll help however I can—that is, if you want my help."

"Of course. I just... why me? Why did you do all of this for me?"

Monroe's arms fell to her side. "No one else has ever seen the real me, and wanted to stay." She cracked a weak smile. "And selfishly, I want more muffins."

"I will make you whatever muffins you want. From now until the end of time, this... it's too much. I don't even have the words for it."

"It's barely enough, given what you've done for me. It's in your name, you know. It's yours. I have no hold over it. It is the property of Wren Jackson, free and clear." She leaned against the door. "You'll have to have the gas and electric checked, they said."

"Sure, fine, fine." Wren trailed her fingertips over the dusty surfaces, her imagination alight with all the ways she would make the place hers. She'd have to decide on a name, a color scheme, business cards... hell, she'd need wholesale quantities of ingredients, too, and insurance, but that would all come in time, it was hers, and everything felt so bright that she might burst. "Thank you," she whispered.

"Merry Christmas. Although, full disclosure, I did get you something else, too, but it's small and you'll have to wait for December twenty-fifth."

"This doesn't even feel real."

"It is real," Monroe said, wrapping her in a warm, tight embrace before kissing her again. "What's realer is that you're going to be late if we don't get you to work."

Chapter 20

"What do you think?" Cat asked. "You ready?"

"No," Monroe answered. "I don't think I've ever been less ready."

"Andie is on standby in case we need her, but I have a feeling we'll be just fine." Cat bounced on the balls of her feet, stretching her arms over her head. "Let's go."

They headed off into the thick mass of conifers, the needles a stubborn green against a bleak landscape of old snow and muddy undergrowth. The moon was rising, huge and impenetrable, over the horizon. Monroe's muscles were tensing, pulsing with energy, the pain threatening from just beyond the veil of humanity. "I can feel that it's going to be a bad one."

"Stop fighting it. I can feel you fighting it from here. Just relax."

"If I relax, I'll shift."

"Okay, then shift," Cat said, tying her bag to a low branch.

"But the moon isn't even—"

"Let it happen. Even if it's twenty minutes early, even if it feels like the wrong time."

"But what if something bad happens?"

"It won't."

Monroe huffed quietly. "You can't know that."

"What's the worst thing that's ever happened to you during a shift?"

"My parents locked me in the garage."

"Your parents suck. No one is locking you up." Cat unwrapped a granola bar and ate it in two bites. "Want one? I have spares."

"No, thanks, I brought muffins." She held the bag of leftover baked goods aloft before eating one." What's the worst thing that happened to *you* during a shift?"

"Poachers."

"Yikes."

"I can guarantee they won't be doing that anymore." Cat unwrapped a second granola bar before adding, "I didn't kill them. Andie got them on film."

"Are you still... *you*, when you shift?"

"Mostly. Are you?"

Monroe nodded. "Mostly," she agreed. Pin pricks danced across her skin, and she braced for the impact of the shift.

"Cold tonight," Cat said, undressing behind a dense bush, folding her clothes into the suspended bag. "I love the crisp air, don't you?"

"I'm scared," Monroe admitted, slowly unbuttoning her shirt. "It always hurts."

"Tell me when you start feeling that weird buzzing in your spine."

Monroe finished undressing, standing in the snow. She'd be glad for a fur coat. "It started."

"What works for me is leaning against a tree and picturing myself as a Bear. For my sister, it's being on all fours. For the boys, it's being curled up like they were in a den."

"Okay." She leaned against the tree, but that felt awkward. She tried all fours, and then curling up. "None of that feels natural."

"What does feel natural?"

Monroe sat on the hard ground, her hands pressing into the dirt in front of her. "Okay, I think this feels alright."

"Close your eyes. Imagine the form you take. Feel that crackling energy in the air, that lunar shift, pulling us gently into the current."

"I feel like I'm losing control."

"Then lose control. This is your time to be free."

Monroe did as she was told, closing her eyes and picturing the Bear within. She was braced for the pain to come, at first. She waited for it to slam into her, to drag a tortured whimper from her mouth, but it never came. When she opened her eyes again, she was already shifted. She breathed deep the sharp piney scent of the woods, mottled with decaying wood and a stream somewhere nearby, and followed the other Bear to the water, where she drank the cleanest, crispest water she had ever tasted.

* * *

Monroe emerged from the woods the next morning, clad in her muddied sweatshirt and tracksuit bottoms, followed by Cat. "That was... different."

"Good different?" Cat asked.

"It's going to take some getting used to."

"Yeah, it will."

"Thank you for helping me."

Cat clapped a hand on Monroe's shoulder. "Not many of us around anymore, you know? I probably still would have helped, even if you were *really* annoying."

"Gee, thanks."

"You aren't, though."

"Sure, that's what you say now."

"Andie said that you bought a bakery?" Cat prodded.

Monroe laughed. "Clearly Jaime can't keep a secret. I did buy a bakery, but it's for Wren."

"Are you sticking around Roanoak Falls, then, or am I going to have to chase you across the country to make sure you aren't trying to slide past lunar cycles?"

"I'll be here until they get sick of me."

"Hey. You're a good person, Monroe Chase. You need to stop talking yourself down. You're fun, and you're loyal. Anyone can see that."

Monroe coughed, trying to change the subject. "I wonder if the voting results are in."

"Won't have to wonder too long. Looks like we have a welcoming party." Andie and Wren were waiting by Andie's car, waving.

"Hey, how did it go?" Wren asked, throwing her arms around Monroe's neck. "You look... well?"

"I feel tired, but okay."

"I feel like I could eat seventeen stacks of pancakes," Cat said, slapping her stomach. "Let's go to that diner."

* * *

The table was already littered with stacked plates and half-empty mugs of coffee when Jaime skidded into the diner, waving the morning paper.

"Look!" they shouted, thrusting the newspaper at Wren. "Mr. Ranelli won!"

"Oh wow," Wren breathed. "I almost can't believe we actually did it."

"No news of Syndicorp's involvement?" Monroe prompted.

"The district attorney heard about the bribes, and Amber Pennington is being indicted. Syndicorp's name was left off of the paperwork, however."

"Typical."

"A win is still a win," Jaime said in a triumphant tone. "Mr. Ranelli cried when I told him. Said he never thought it was possible. Also said he heard about the bakery. He's happy for you, Wren."

Monroe sat back in the worn booth, looking out at the forest in the distance, framing a beautiful town that she was learning to call home. It was, after all, the place that was teaching her to know peace.

Epilogue

"This month, another Bear joined our family," Cat announced, her half-full glass lifted high over the table. "I feel grateful to know you, Monroe Chase."

"I'm lucky you showed up," Monroe said, rubbing her side where the fur once was, now receded into human skin. "I'm lucky in all the ways I never was before."

"From our family to this new one, Merry Damn Christmas," Cat said, gesturing around at her sister, the boys, and Delilah, who was giggling into a tall mug of hot chocolate, whipped cream on her nose. "I'm glad we could all be together. Sometimes, you find a family in the oddest places."

"I'd say that again," Jaime said, after drinking a swig of their wine. "Never thought I'd be beset on all sides by Bears. Can't say I'm complaining, though, it sure makes for a nice Christmas. To the chef!" they said, sloshing wine out of their glass as Daisy the chinchilla rustled happily in her cage against the wall.

Wren stood and gave a deep bow. "It was my pleasure, but I'll have each and every one of you know that I'm not washing a single dish."

"I volunteer," Monroe said, already collecting the empty plates. "Besides, there's still dessert." She bent and kissed Wren on the top of the head, lingering there just a moment. "I hear it's pecan pie. My favorite."

"And to new beginnings," Andie added, holding her can of beer aloft. "New beginnings of all kinds."

"I can't wait to start at the bakery," Wren said. "And with Monroe and Jaime on my team, it feels exciting, and sparkly, and new—and making a wedding cake in the spring is the perfect start to a grand opening."

"Damn right," Cat said, a little tipsy, planting a kiss on Andie. "Sparkly and new, that's what we all need."

Monroe turned on the ambient lights as she exited the room, now that the evening was drawing in. Still, even in the deep golden glow of twilight, the snowflakes falling glittered, perching quietly on growing snow drifts. Roanoak Falls was home.

The end

Keep reading for a sneak peek into book 2 of the Midwest Weres series, Bearly Together!

Sign up for my newsletter and get information about convention appearances, book launch parties, new releases, and more! Get bonus content for the Cricket Chronicles series like deleted scenes and extended cuts. You can unsubscribe at any time with no obligation.

http://eepurl.com/gOQBaP

FOLLOW ME

You can follow me on Twitter at @IMRyannFletcher, on Facebook @RyannFletcherWrites, Instagram @RyannFletcherWrites, or email at RyannFletcherBooks@Gmail.com. It's always great to hear from you!

Polar Opposites preview

Snow sparkled against the distant, sloped peak, the mid-morning sun reflecting off the mountain and down onto the road that approached the lodge. Max flipped down the visor, flinching from the receipt she forgot she'd stashed up there at the last stop for gas, an expensive tank she'd had to put on her credit card. One more mile to the lodge and she could collapse into her cabin. There was a time she could have done a six hour drive with no problem, but that was before she'd found herself alone in the front seat.

Static hissed from the radio, and she twisted the knob to turn it off. The lodge was too far from a radio tower, and the land was too hilly up here to get any kind of decent signal. She'd be living off whatever music she'd remembered to pile onto her phone until the end of the winter break season, and in that exact moment, she remembered that she'd forgotten to transfer the files. They were organized neatly by artist and genre, in folders sitting untouched on the desktop of her computer, a few hundred miles to the south.

Max groaned, lightly smacking the steering wheel as she pulled into the lodge's driveway. It was the same as it had been the previous year, and the year before that, as long as she'd been going to Crimson Oak. She parked, climbing out of the driver's seat and slamming the lightly rusted door behind her. Checking her reflection in the side mirror, she bent to examine a stray lock of short, dark hair springing from the back. She frowned and pressed it down, ruffling her pixie cut in the process.

It was unusually warm for the start of the season, with no snow except at the peak of Bear Mountain. Her lined boots were heavy and hot, and she was regretting not packing something else.

"Checking in," she said, pushing through the door of reception. Bells tied to the top jingled lightly as she stepped over the threshold, blinking into the relative darkness. "Max Carter, instructor."

"Max!" Orren yelled. "You're back!"

Her eyes adjusted, and she smiled, leaning against the desk. He looked the same as he always had, his dark skin unblemished, unwrinkled, despite the fact he easily had twenty years on her. Max grinned at him, flashing a smile. "It's me, in the flesh."

"Nice to see you again. Same as last year?"

"Unless Mr. Parker found it in his heart to give us all a nice big raise."

Orren rolled his eyes. "Yeah, as if there's any chance of that happening. I'm surprised any of us are even here this year, with this weather we've been having."

"Yeah, it's a little warm, Orr. Where are you keeping all the snow?"

"My back pocket, obviously." He slid a stack of forms across the desk, secured by three silver paper clips. "The usual."

"Yeah, yeah." Max signed each form, one after another, with her tiny, cramped scrawl of a signature, barely legible but definitely unique. "Anyone else arrive yet?"

"It's just you this year, Max."

She put the pen down. "What?"

Orren shrugged. "Snowboarding program got cut, didn't they tell you? Mr. Parker is on the ropes with this place, some big conglomerate wants to buy the lodge. He's probably going to take the bait, but he wants to juice profits first. It will get a better price that way."

"Oh." Max swallowed hard, the realization sinking into her gut like a stone. "So this is probably the last year for all of us, then."

"He said the new owners agreed to keep on as much staff as they could."

"We all know what that means." Max sighed, picking up the pen to sign the remaining forms. "What about ski instructors, then?"

"They're flying in some hotshot from the Rockies. She almost went national, I hear."

"So only two instructors, one for ski, one for snowboarding?"

"That's not all," Orren said apologetically. "Mr. Parker said whichever program performs worse gets the boot mid-season."

Max smacked her palm against the desk. "What? Why?"

"Same reason. Less staffing costs means bigger profits, and there haven't exactly been tons of people booking trips, not with the weather being what it is. Mr. Parker—"

"Mr. Parker wants to get as big a payout he can, and to hell with the rest of us," Max snarled. "If I had known before I drove up, I wouldn't have even bothered."

"That's a lie, and we both know it," Orren said lightly, taking the signed forms back and straightening them. "You couldn't stay off this mountain if your life depended on it."

"So what kind of occupancy are we looking at, here? Half?"

"A quarter."

Max gave a low whistle, leaning forward against the desk. "Ouch."

"Might get better by next week, you know the start of December is always more of a jumpstart for the season. It's early, yet, for here."

"We'd better hope so, or he'll have this lodge functioning as a ghost town until the sale is done."

The door's bells jingled once more, and Max turned, an eyebrow raised at the perfectly coiffed, perfectly matching, perfectly composed skier, who looked like she'd stepped right out of Winter Sports magazine. She flipped her shoulder-length hair over her shoulder as though she was already in a photo shoot.

"Sloane Hearst, checking in."

"Ah, Ms. Hearst," Orren said, flipping through a stack of papers. "You're our new ski instructor."

"This mountain isn't very impressive, is it?" Sloane said, arms folded over her chest. "I've seen bunny slopes with a steeper grade."

Max laughed. "Trust me, the trails up there are more of a challenge than they first seem. Lots of little jumps, obstacles, and there's the ski jump on the other side." She held out her hand. "Max Carter. I'm the snowboard instructor."

"I didn't know they offered snowboarding here."

Max pulled her hand back. She recognized that tone, that lightly dismissive way of addressing her. Damned skiers. "They have for a number of years now. I'm sorry that your cursory internet search failed to tell you that."

"Given I was pulled in at the last minute to boost the lodge's attendance, I didn't have much time to scope things out." Sloane removed her thin gloves, stashing them in her pockets. "Clearly their snowboard instructor wasn't quite pulling in the numbers."

"I'll have you know that I grew this program from nothing," Max snapped. "Who even are you, Sloane Hearst? Some up-jumped ski fanatic who almost went national, but couldn't quite hack it? Wow, what a legacy, to almost have been someone important."

Orren cleared his throat. "Alright, then," he said, sliding a stack of papers to Sloane. "Max, it's the same as last year, if you want to go settle in." Max opened her mouth to let another snide remark loose, but he shot her a warning look, and she put her hands up in surrender.

"Whatever. You know where to find me if you need me. When's first lesson?"

"You're booked in for ten tomorrow morning." He slid a thick folder across the desk. "Your lanyard and tags are all in here, should be everything you need, I'd imagine. You've been here long enough, you know the ropes."

"What's the deal with food this year?"

"Same as last year, you can pick up leftovers from the back of the kitchen. Reduced staff this year, though, so—"

Max rolled her eyes. "Yeah. Of course."

"Linens are in bags by the door," Orren said with a nod. "Same as always, you can get the laundry machines for two hours on Sundays between changeovers."

"Roger that," she replied, hefting the canvas bag over her shoulder. "Did they ever get that messed up washing machine fixed from last year? Wringing out my clothes by hand got real old after a couple of weeks."

Orren grimaced apologetically, waving an arm at her. "You know how it is." He tugged at his plaid jacket, adjusting the zipper that ran from one shoulder to the opposite hip. "If you get there early, you'll be able to grab the good machine. Might be easier this year with less staff?"

"Silver linings," Max replied with another eye roll. She shot a look at the ski instructor and her rigid posture before she opened the door. "I'll come by in the morning for my schedule, Orren."

He waved at her, and she adjusted the weight of the canvas bag, distributing it over her shoulder. Gravel crunched under her boots as she walked back to her small utility vehicle, frowning at the amount of mud caked along the underside. It was too wet for late November. Too much rain, not enough snow, and the mountain would be even more treacherous than it usually was.

That ski instructor would learn soon enough that Bear Mountain wasn't as tame as it appeared. Max checked the calendar on her phone. The full moon was in three days, and she was already yearning for the icy air of the summit.

About the Author

Huge thanks to my wife, who never fails to amaze me with her dedication to my books. Without her, these characters wouldn't exist.

Thanks as well to my writing buddies, who help break the monotony of formatting with hilarious anecdotes and kind words.

Ryann Fletcher is a writer who lives with her wife and too many craft supplies. She writes sapphic science fiction and fantasy, and likes to cook.

You can connect with me on:
- https://ryannfletcher.com
- https://twitter.com/IMRyannFletcher
- https://facebook.com/RyannFletcherWrites
- https://instagram.com/RyannFletcherWrites
- https://www.tiktok.com/@ryannfletcherwrites

Subscribe to my newsletter:
- http://eepurl.com/gOQBaP

Also by Ryann Fletcher

Polar Opposites – Midwest Weres book 3

https://books2read.com/Polar-Opposites

Maxine has dedicated her life to snowboarding. When she learns that this winter may be her last season as an instructor, she's forced to compete with a high-profile athlete while she's trying to chase poachers off the mountain.

Fresh from a crushing defeat, Sloane takes a job as an instructor. What she didn't expect was having to battle a rival alongside her Bear shifting, which could explose her kind to the world.

With the future of the lodge on the line, will Max and Sloane learn to work together - or will they let their differences get the better of them?

www.ingramcontent.com/pod-product-compliance
Lightning Source LLC
Chambersburg PA
CBHW021729190726
48288CB00009B/2974